WITCH IN A CRISIS

A BLAIR WILKES MYSTERY

ELLE ADAMS

I looked at the scrap of paper in my hand, rereading the words for what felt like the millionth time.

Blair Wilkes. I heard about your involvement in recent events in your home of Fairy Falls. Have you rethought your decision to turn down my offer of employment?

The Inquisitor.

Two weeks on, and the words were still burned into my brain. The fact that the leader of the paranormal hunters wanted to hire the likes of me—a fairy witch who happened to be the daughter of two convicted criminals—felt more of a threat than a job offer. Even so, I hardly believed the Inquisitor still thought I'd accept his offer after everything he'd done to the people I cared about. My parents, I was convinced, had been set up by the very person who'd written this note, which had ended with my mother dead and my father jailed for life.

Alissa, my flatmate, walked into the living room and eyed the note in my hand. "Why do you still have that thing?"

I gave a shrug. "I hoped if I looked at it long enough, I'd stop being scared of him."

"Miaow," said Sky, my familiar, hopping onto the sofa next to me. The little black cat blinked one blue eye and one grey one, and batted the note out of my hand with his single white paw.

"There, see?" said Alissa. "He knows."

I scooped up the note and put it down on the arm of the sofa. "I don't know if he expects me to reply. It's not like I have the Inquisitor's private address, and I'm not letting that poor pixie near him again."

"He has some nerve even trying to get to you," she responded. "He must know you're aware of what he is now."

"I think he is," I said. "I also think he's testing me."

The Inquisitor was a fairy, and while I hadn't known it the first time we'd met, there was absolutely no way he didn't know I'd figured it out by now. He'd pretty much placed the evidence in front of me, though he was using a permanent glamour to fool everyone around him into thinking he was human, utterly ordinary and non-magical. Even my ability to sense what type of paranormal someone was hadn't managed to see through his act, and it'd taken months for me to put the pieces together. I still didn't know if the rest of the hunters were aware of his true nature, but considering he was in a position of authority among a group of people with a notorious disdain for paranormals, it seemed highly unlikely they knew what he was.

"Don't let him play head games with you," said Alissa. "He left you that note to get a reaction from you, that's all. Listen to my grandmother."

I smiled. "Yeah, that's always wise advice."

Alissa was the granddaughter of the town's coven leader, and Madame Grey was one of the smartest and toughest witches I knew. Yet despite all that, the Inquisitor wasn't to be trifled with, and against my better judgement, I was planning on doing exactly that.

The winged form of the pixie flew around my head, and Sky swatted at him. I gave my familiar a stern look. "Stop that."

"Miaow," he grumbled, as displeased by the little fairy's presence as ever. The pixie had moved in here after narrowly escaping whoever had sent him with the Inquisitor's message, and I'd promised to keep him safe from harm. At this rate, my cat would be more of a danger to him than the hunters would, though. The pixie was about eight inches tall with blond tufty hair and pointed ears and spent most of his time hiding, yet my cat was *not* impressed by the fact that our entire flat was now covered in glitter. In fairness, I found it a little annoying, too, but half the glitter probably came from my own habit of switching between human and fairy forms, so I couldn't blame it all on the pixie.

"I know I should get rid of the note." I crumpled the scrap of paper in my hand. "I'm just worried about Nathan."

"I don't blame you, but he knows what he's doing," Alissa said in soothing tones. "Besides, he's visiting family, not storming the Lancashire Prison for Paranormals."

I checked my phone. "Yeah, but he was supposed to be back any minute now—"

The doorbell rang. I was on my feet an instant later. Nathan, my boyfriend, happened to be an ex-paranormal hunter himself, and he'd been running a particularly risky mission for me over the weekend. He was the only person in my life who might have been able to help me get hold of the means to contact my dad in the hunters' jail, and I'd been on tenterhooks waiting to find out if he'd succeeded without being jailed himself.

Relief flooded me when I opened the door and found Nathan standing on the doorstep, looking tired. His dark hair had grown a little longer in the last few weeks, while his jacket was stained with mud and so were his hiking trousers. He gave me a smile and greeted me with a kiss.

"You're all right?" I said.

"Of course," he said. "I'm not late, am I?"

"Only by about five minutes." I stepped back to let him into the flat. Normally, I wouldn't have worried about a short delay, but he'd been on more than just a visit to his family's home. After all, most of his family were active or retired paranormal hunters when the leader of said hunters was trying to blackmail me at this very moment. Nathan had taken a major risk in going back to his dad's house to look for the Pixie-Glass, and judging from the fact that he'd returned empty-handed, he hadn't been able to find it.

Should have known it wouldn't be that easy. A Pixie-Glass —a magical item of which there was a grand total of one present in the region—was the only way to communicate with someone incarcerated in the hunters' most secure jail. Since the Pixie-Glass in question was in the possession of no other than Nathan's father, who had no liking for me whatsoever, we'd been forced into a corner.

We went into the living room, where Alissa stood in the kitchen area brewing tea for all three of us. The pixie flew out of sight when Nathan walked in, still nervous around strangers. Alissa's familiar, Roald, mewed a greeting from the corner, while Sky hopped onto the sofa in the spot where I'd been sitting.

"I have good news and bad news," said Nathan. "The bad news is that I didn't manage to find the Pixie-Glass."

I exhaled in a sigh. I couldn't say I'd expected it would be that easy. "And the good news?"

He held up a thick wad of paper in answer, bound in a cardboard folder.

"What's that?" I asked.

"The documents from your father's trial," he said. "I managed to grab it without being suspected."

"You did?" My heart gave a lurch, then began to beat faster. "Are you sure you're allowed to have that?"

"Relax, Blair," he said. "My dad won't know it's gone. I doubt he would ever suspect we're planning to contact the LPFP."

No, it was the Inquisitor whose eyes I felt watching me from a distance. Nathan's dad had been the last person to speak to my mother alive and had been disdainful towards me from the moment we'd met, but compared to the Inquisitor, he posed no threat to me.

Besides, Nathan and his father couldn't be more different. When I'd told him my suspicions about the Inquisitor, he'd believed me without question, but even being an ex-hunter didn't put him in a position to challenge the guy in charge. I was grateful beyond words for his choice to help me find out what had really happened to my dad.

I doubted the hunters had arrested my dad on genuine charges, so it was time to find out what crime he'd been accused of. Something serious enough to warrant him being locked up in one of the most secure paranormal prisons in the country, yet not something they'd made available as public information. With the file in my hands, I'd be better equipped to figure out how to expose the truth and get my dad freed. Without getting arrested myself. *No pressure, Blair.*

I sat down on the sofa, and Sky hopped into my lap and curled up. "All right, tell me the worst."

Nathan cleared his throat. "The document states that your father was found to have stolen a priceless artefact which belonged to the regional witch council of the northwest. He was jailed for life after a trial in front of the hunters."

My mouth parted. "He stole from the *witches?*"

"Apparently," he said. "Not any coven in Fairy Falls, but the regional council and their headquarters up in Carlisle. I'm not clear on what exactly a Seeing Stone is, but it's valuable enough to warrant a lifelong jail sentence."

Alissa turned around, the kettle in her hand. "That sounds dodgy to me. Nothing the regional council owns ought to be worth *that* level of punishment."

"Yeah," I said. "Did the files mention my mother at all?"

"No," said Nathan. "I'm sorry, Blair."

A lump grew in my throat. My mother was dead, killed by the same people who'd pursued my father, and it'd taken me a while to accept that the hunters and the fairies were one and the same. But the *witches?* I'd never have guessed that they might have been involved in the sentence passed on my dad. They must know he was innocent. He'd have no reason to steal from the region's witch council, right?

"What's a Seeing Stone?" I asked. "I've never heard of one before."

"Haven't a clue," Alissa said. "Madame Grey will know."

I didn't doubt that, but my old fears came back at the thought of everyone I cared about potentially being dragged into this mess. I'd come far too close to losing everything at the hands of the hunters on more than one occasion, and every time, it had been Inquisitor Hare who'd been pulling the strings. How had he talked the witch council into condemning a man to a lifetime in the most secure prison in the region for stealing something he probably couldn't even use? I mean, he wasn't a witch, and my mum had been dead by that point.

"She will." Nathan gave Sky a stroke as the little cat padded over to him, meowing in such a way that meant, *Thanks for not getting arrested.* Or possibly, *Blair was worried about you, and now you have to pay for it by giving me attention all evening.* Being Sky, it was anyone's guess.

Alissa walked over with three mugs of tea, which she distributed among us. "We can ask her. She'll be able to speak to the regional witch council herself; she meets with them all the time."

"Yeah." I put my mug down on the coffee table. "To be honest, it reminds me of the sceptre incident all over again. Except I'm sure Aveline Hollyhock would have told everyone in town if she knew my dad had been arrested for stealing from the witches."

My mum had temporarily stolen the sceptre belonging to the local Head Witch in order to protect me, but as far as I knew, my dad hadn't been involved in that particular theft. Not that I knew for sure, since I had no way to contact him directly.

"We'll talk to her," Nathan said. "I'm sure she'll be willing to help. She already offered to do everything she could to prepare for the Inquisitor's arrival, right?"

"She will." I picked up my tea and sipped, noting that Alissa had put in a pinch of calming tonic. "I just hope the other witches will be as cooperative when it comes down to it. At least some of the council must have agreed with the hunters' verdict, otherwise they'd never have been able to get away with it."

"Not necessarily," Nathan said. "You can borrow the files to read if you like, but I'll have to return them to my father's house soon before he realises they're missing."

"We can always make a copy." I put down my mug. "Using a spell. I haven't got to that stage in my lessons yet, but it's do-able, right?"

Alissa nodded, pulling out her wand. "I can do that."

She waved her wand, and an identical copy of the cardboard file appeared next to me on the sofa. I handed the original file back to Nathan and picked up the copy. The name on the cover read, 'Braden Eventide'. A jolt of emotion hit me.

"That's his name," I murmured to myself. "Braden Eventide."

"Huh?" said Alissa.

I raised my head. "I didn't know my dad's name. Remember when I tried to talk to those fairies about him and they didn't know who he was? He never signed his notes, but..."

"That's the name he gave," said Nathan, slipping the other file into his coat.

"Braden Eventide." I tried out the name. "So I guess I could have been Blair Eventide, or Blair Wildflower."

Nathan put a hand on my arm. "You can read the file later. Then we can decide our next move."

"Thanks for getting it for me." I drank the rest of my tea and waved my wand to levitate the mug over to the sink. "I appreciate you taking the risk."

"My dad was hardly going to have me locked up for paying him a visit," he said. "Want to go to the Troll's Tavern? We can talk about our next move while we're there."

"That sounds perfect."

I went to get ready for our date to our favourite pub in town, feeling bolstered despite the lingering worries over my dad's arrest. Nathan had done his best for me even with his family being set against us from the start. Regardless of all the obstacles the universe had thrown into our paths, the two of us had been able to build a relationship together. If we could do that, we could save my dad, right?

Okay, not all his family hated me. His sister, Erin, had become one of my close friends, though she'd quit the hunters and now lived in Fairy Falls with her fiancé, Buck, who was also half-fairy like me. Both of us had been glamoured by our fairy parents before we'd entered the magical world—in my case, my parents, before they'd put me into foster care in the normal world to keep me safe. Buck, on the other hand, had been recruited to join the hunters directly. He'd only quit when his fiancée had chosen to do so, and while he remained on the reserve team, both he and Erin had offered to stand beside me along with Nathan. Against their own family, if necessary.

No wonder Nathan's dad wasn't a fan of me. I figured Erin would have left the hunters anyway, but I'd likely expedited her decision. At the time, I hadn't known that Nathan's dad owned the only Pixie-Glass in the area except for the one which belonged to Blythe's mother. Since Mrs Dailey had taken hers with her to the same jail my dad was incarcerated in, we were unlikely to be able to use it, which meant I had to figure out where Nathan's dad had hidden his own.

Yet unless we figured out how to prove my dad's innocence, it probably wasn't worth the risk of incurring the wrath of the local hunters' branch by stealing the glass from them. Instead, I'd read through the notes on the trial later tonight, and then I'd go to speak to Madame Grey tomorrow, and she'd help me figure out how to get in touch with the northwest's regional witch council.

It all sounded easy enough on paper, but a flicker of worry stirred inside me at the thought of any of the witches being involved in his capture. Not just the hunters or even the fairies, but the witches, the group of people who'd welcomed me into the magical world from the start. The people I'd come to trust. How could I believe they'd been involved in jailing my dad and exiling me from the magical community at large?

Admittedly, Blythe and her mother were also witches and they'd hated me from the get-go, but they hadn't been popular among their fellow witches even before Mrs Dailey had wound up jailed for scheming against Madame Grey. They were also my distant relations, not that they thought of themselves as such. To be fair, Blythe hadn't been unfriendly the last time we'd spoken to one another. In fact, she'd implied she supported my desire to free my dad from jail. I doubted she'd lay her life on the line for me, though. She didn't believe it was possible to outwit the hunters, and who knew, maybe it wasn't. Yet Nathan had my back, and my friends did, too. They'd promised to help me rescue my dad, and I was closer to that goal than ever before.

My gaze caught on a photo on the bedside table, and I studied the image of my mother which I'd taken from Blythe's house. Tanith Wildflower had long dark curly hair, pale skin, a smile that mirrored my own. She'd died to protect me, and my dad… he'd paid the price for both of us.

If I didn't find a way to prove my dad's innocence, the hunters would do to him what they'd done to countless other people and leave him in jail for the rest of his life. I would never let that happen. Never.

2

Needless to say, it was difficult for me to get into the right headspace to focus on work the next morning. Nathan and I had stayed out at the pub for most of the previous evening, talking over our options, and I'd slept in too late to go to see the witches first thing in the morning. That meant I had to wait until my magic lesson that evening to ask Madame Grey what she knew of my dad's supposed crime.

There was never a dull moment at Dritch & Co, the paranormal recruitment firm where I'd worked for the better half of the past year. From unicorn handlers to wand makers, goblin markets and even a dead body in the cupboard on one occasion—you could always count on Dritch & Co to be at the centre of the action here in Fairy Falls. It had always attracted a high level of mayhem even by the magical world's standards, and things had only escalated after my arrival in town.

My co-workers included Bethan, daughter of the boss and the single fastest, most efficient worker I'd seen. Tall and lean, she had endless energy and was constantly on the move. There was also Rob the muscular blond were-wolf, who was the most personable of our group. And then there was Lizzie, who wore her hair in a barrette today, and was in the middle of fixing the printer as I entered the room. She'd built the printer herself, along with the coffee machine, which made them a little more active than most typical office equipment. It also explained the printer's habit of breaking into song or throwing ink at people it didn't like.

"How's life, Blair?" asked Bethan. "You're being quiet."

"Just trying to figure out how to deal with this client," I said vaguely.

My co-workers didn't know all the details of my chaotic family life, though it was hard to keep it from affecting my workload when my head was in the clouds at the best of times after all the upheavals I'd faced recently. I scanned the list of clients for the day and the names slid straight out of my brain as soon as I read them.

Luckily, the universe decided to spare me. No sooner had I picked up the phone than my boss walked in. Veronica Eldritch and her daughter looked similar enough to be mistaken for sisters, except the former's hair was white instead of black. The same manic energy surrounded both of them, which, when I was already tired, made me want to lie down for a nap. "Blair, a word, please."

I hoped it wasn't bad news, but I didn't know how much the boss knew about my recent discoveries or the Inquisitor's sudden interest in hiring me again. Maybe nothing at all. She liked to check in with me about my progress in learning magic, but the only people who knew of my feud with the hunters were Alissa, Nathan and his family, and Madame Grey. Oh, and Blythe knew some of it, too. She'd once worked for Dritch & Co herself and blamed me for getting her fired, which had only been the beginning of our contentious relationship. I'd come a long way from having a minor breakdown on the floor on my first day here after being confronted with the magical world for the first time, but being called to the boss's office always made me wary. And not just because of the one time we'd found a dead body in there.

Callie, the receptionist, waved at me as I walked to the boss's office, which changed appearance depending on Veronica's whims. Today, the interior was set out like a glade in a forest, complete with an array of plants growing around the desk and between the filing cabinets. Birds flitted overhead, trilling in my ears, while the hum of insects filled the background along with the fragrant smell of flowers. It was a bit distracting; I'd say that much. I took a seat on a tree stump which had replaced the chair I usually sat in, while Veronica faced me across a desk which now had a vine-covered computer sitting on it.

"How're things, Blair?" she asked.

"Um, fine," I lied. My boss didn't need to know I'd unintentionally drawn the attention of the Inquisitor of the paranormal hunters. Work was one of the few 'normal' parts of my life I had left. Which, given the eccentricities of our clients, said something about how weird everything else was lately.

"Good," said Veronica. "I'm glad to hear it. I know you've had a difficult time recently."

Had she been talking to Madame Grey? Maybe. My boss wasn't actively involved with the coven who ran the town, but she'd been at school at the same time as my mother, though they hadn't known each other that well. By now, though, half the town knew at least the basics of my bizarre family history.

"I'm fine," I repeated, wondering who I thought I was kidding.

Veronica nodded. "Yes, of course. If you're sure you can focus on the job, I need someone to deal with an employer looking for three people to clean up after his pet manticore. You can handle that, can't you, Blair?"

"Um…"

A pile of files materialised in my hands. Guess I'd asked for that one. Maybe I should have said I was suffering terrible angst instead.

"And three broomstick-cleaners." Three more files appeared, as I struggled to get my grip on the stack of papers. "And a new client who wants to find someone to test fifteen versions of a new patent on Seven-League Boots."

"Um—" A new stack of files appeared on top of the heap, wobbling a little. "Thanks."

I backed out of the office before Veronica could throw any more files at me. *Never a dull moment indeed.*

———

"Concentrate," Rita said, as I aimed my wand at Rebecca. "Really, Blair. Are you incapable of pointing your wand in a straight line?"

Possibly. Rebecca's ginger cat familiar, Toast, meowed at me from the desk as though adding his admonishment. He usually stayed out of our practical classes in case he got hit by a stray spell, which admittedly was more likely to come from me than from Rebecca. Let's just say my technique was still a little unreliable on a good day, and I had so much on my mind that it was a wonder I could hold my *head* upright.

Sure enough, my spell shot past her and hit the wall, causing a bright sparkling substance to appear all over the plaster.

Rita tutted at me. "That's glitter, not glue, Blair. Unless your opponent has a glitter phobia, I doubt it'll discourage them."

"You never know," I said. "Some people hate glitter."

Rebecca gave me an encouraging grin. She and I took magic lessons together every week, and we'd made the mutual decision to opt to accelerate our lessons in magical self-defence. Rebecca, who also happened to be the younger sister of my former nemesis, Blythe, had unexpectedly gained the title of the region's Head Witch after the ceremonial sceptre had chosen her to wield it. Considering she was only eleven, this turn of events had come as a shock to everyone, including Rebecca herself. As a result, everyone had agreed that it was pertinent that she learn how to defend herself as quickly as possible. Such defence classes were best taken with another person, and I attracted enough trouble on a daily basis that I had zero problem with being moved to the same programme as Rebecca. Unfortunately, mastering tricky defensive spells required more focus than I had to give at the moment.

"You're aiming too far to the right," said Rita. "Try again."

"Sure." I adjusted my grip and fired off another spell.

Rebecca deflected it with a wave of her wand, and a few handfuls of glitter fell to the ground.

"Better," said Rita. "Now try using the sceptre, Rebecca."

Rebecca put down her wand and picked up the sceptre, which was longer than her arm. It had taken some adjusting for her to be able to use it like a wand and she still tripped up sometimes, especially given her lack of experience at magic in general. She'd fallen behind her peers on her magical training due to her scheming mother keeping her at home to exploit her talent at altering people's personalities by looking them in the eye. Since I was also several leagues behind other witches of my age, we made a good team, and we'd both made big strides in our progress since we'd started taking lessons together several months ago.

Now her mother was safely ensconced in jail, but the witches kept a close watch on Rebecca in case anyone else tried to take advantage of her position as Head Witch. Like, say, the paranormal hunters. I had to admit that glitter wouldn't be much help against any of them—or the Inquisitor, for that matter—though I'd rather avoid a direct confrontation with *him* if I could avoid it. A duel with the Inquisitor wasn't a fight I could win, no matter how much progress I'd made at learning magic.

I waved my wand at Rebecca. This time, she deflected the spell with a powerful shield, sending it bouncing straight back at me. I flew into the air, a sticky substance covering my arms and legs like I'd jumped into a pool full of slime.

"Oops." Rebecca waved her wand and the slime vanished. "Got carried away."

"At least you got the spell right," said Rita. "Next time, Blair, do try to defend yourself. You know how to disable a shielding spell by now."

I retrieved my wand from where I'd dropped it, my face heating. My sense of focus went out of the window in times of stress, and it seemed like my life consisted of a never-ending series of upheavals lately.

"You're still distracted," she commented. "Both of you, but especially you, Blair."

I hung my head. "Sorry. I've had a lot on my mind this week. I'll try again."

As we got into position, Rebecca whispered, "Are you okay?"

I nodded. "Sure."

From her expression, I had an inkling she knew something more was going on than simple difficulty mastering a spell. She was observant and smart, and far more mature than the average eleven-year-old. Being able to mess with people's personalities by looking at them tended to have that effect, and so did growing up with a scheming mother like Mrs Dailey.

Witches usually had one major talent, and Rebecca's was powerful enough to give even the former Head Witch a run for her money. Mine was a weird combination of both my parents', enabling me to sense truth from lies and tell what paranormal type someone was by looking at them. As for regular magic, I was currently on Grade Four, making me as talented as the average nine-year-old. I'd be at this stage for a while, though I was now learning basic magical history and other topics in theory lessons as well as taking practical classes with Rebecca.

And then there was fairy magic, for which I didn't

have a tutor. Unless you counted the pixie, though my cat had given me a few 'lessons', too. I could snap my fingers and turn myself invisible, as well as adjusting my glamour to imitate anyone else. Yet I still felt inadequate compared to the other fairies I'd met.

Especially the Inquisitor.

Asking for a lesson in fairy magic from Rita wouldn't do any good, so I did my best to bring my attention back to the present for the duration of the lesson.

When we finished, Rebecca and I walked outside the classroom and into the lobby of the witches' headquarters.

"Can you let your sister know I need to talk to her?" I asked. "As soon as possible."

"Oh, sure," she said. "What're you doing now?"

"I just need to have a word with Rita," I said. "Take care of yourself, okay?"

She left the building, while I released a steadying breath. *It's okay. The witches wouldn't have lied to you about helping the hunters imprison your father.* Not Rita, anyway. Nor Madame Grey.

I ducked back into the classroom, where Rita gave me an expectant look. "Are you going to tell me what's on your mind?"

"It's my dad," I said. "My birth father, that is. Did Madame Grey tell you about the note I got the other week? From—the hunters."

She gave a nod, her mouth pinching. "Yes, she did. You haven't received another note, have you?"

"No, but I found out why my dad was arrested," I told her. "Apparently, he stole something from the regional witch coven, something valuable enough to earn a lifetime sentence in jail. Did you know?"

She frowned. "No. What did he steal?"

"A Seeing Stone," I said. "According to the report, anyway. Nathan found the file detailing my dad's trial at his family's house."

Her brow furrowed. "You asked Nathan to look for the records? Why?"

"Because…" I hesitated. Rita was on my side, I knew, but she was also more of a rule-follower than I was. "Because I wanted to know which crime he'd been convicted of committing, since I didn't know the details, and nobody else seems to know either."

"And now you do," she said. "I'm afraid I don't know anything about your father's case, Blair."

"Maybe not, but—do you know what a Seeing Stone is?" I asked. "Why is it so valuable?"

"I can't say I do," she said. "Madame Grey will know. She was still the leader of the Meadowsweet Coven at the time of your dad's arrest, and she had a prominent position on the regional witch council. I didn't."

"I planned to ask her," I said, "but I'm wondering if there was some kind of manipulation involved in his trial. Magical, I mean."

"Ask Madame Grey, if you must assuage your curiosity," she said. "But please don't lose focus on your lessons, Blair. You'll need them."

"I'll try not to," I said, "but I get the feeling the hunters won't take kindly to me ignoring them."

"Yes, well, Madame Grey might believe the town is ready to face the hunters, but I'm less than convinced that standing up to them won't end in disaster for all of us," she said. "We need to be careful not to attract their attention before we're ready. There's no telling what they might do."

"I'll try not to," I said, silently suspecting that I'd had their attention for a long while now. It was only a matter of time before the Inquisitor decided to make his next move.

"Good," said Rita. "I'll see you at your next lesson, Blair."

I left the classroom, heading for Madame Grey's office. She, at least, knew what we were up against. In fact, she'd all but said she expected the hunters to come to town and was preparing for the worst. I didn't want to bring trouble on the covens before they were ready, but at the same time, the need for the truth gnawed at me. My dad was completely at the hunters' mercy, while the Inquisitor's note hadn't had a time limit on it. For all I knew, he might show up for my answer any day now.

Keeping up with my lessons was one thing… but it'd take more than my witch magic to take a stand against the most powerful fairy in the region.

I made my way to Madame Grey's office and knocked on the oak wood door.

3

I knocked again, then twice more. Finally, Madame Grey's voice called from within the office, "Come in."

I opened the door to see Madame Grey put the phone down on her desk. "Oh, sorry I interrupted you."

"No problem." She waved a hand to invite me in, and I closed the door behind me. "What is it, Blair?"

"Nathan went back home to see his father," I said. "He found the report of my dad's arrest, and it sounds like the reason they imprisoned him was because he stole something belonging to the region witch council. The Seeing Stone."

Madame Grey was silent for a moment. "I see. I gather you've probably guessed that I wasn't involved in the trial, or else I would have told you."

"I thought so, but—I want to know why they gave him a life imprisonment for a simple theft." I fiddled with a loose thread on my coat. "If it was a witch who he supposedly stole from, why did they let the hunters dictate the terms of his punishment?"

"Unfortunately, I suspect that it was the hunters who caught him, in which case they would have had total control over how the trial played out," she said. "They'll have had at least one witch from the regional council present at the trial, yes, but the hunters ultimately hold the authority on such matters. They make the laws, after all."

"Because they're supposed to be impartial." A hint of bitterness entered my voice. "Except they're not. Who else would have been involved in the trial? I read the whole file, but I didn't find any mention of any witches."

"I'd be inclined to ask the former Head Witch who was present at the trial, but I don't believe she's taking visitors at the moment," she said. "In any case, I've no doubt that if she'd known your father was trialled for stealing from the regional witch coven, she would have mentioned it during her visit here last year."

I grimaced. "I figured as much."

The former Head Witch, Aveline Hollyhock, had lost her title to none other than Rebecca, and was understandably incensed by that development. Considering she'd also been the world's worst house guest, I wasn't exactly keen to see her again. I doubted she'd been the one who'd sentenced my dad, though, however much she'd known about my mother's thieving exploits.

"I'll give her a call," said Madame Grey. "Failing that, I can draw up a list of witches who were part of the regional council at the time, but it might have been any of them who attended the trial. I'm also not sure they could have overruled the hunters' committee, either, not if every one of the hunters voted in favour of your father's sentence. Generally, the Inquisitor gets the final say. Besides, even if they knew Tanith, they wouldn't have known about the connection between her and your father."

Because none of them knew they had a child together. They didn't know I existed. "What is the Seeing Stone? Why's it so important?"

"The Seeing Stone is a valuable relic similar to the sceptre in that it's belonged to the covens for generations," she said. "Effectively, it's like a more accurate version of a crystal ball, which offers genuine insight into the future. Each of the regions' councils possesses one."

Why would my dad steal that? Couldn't he have just used a regular crystal ball if he wanted to see the future for whatever reason? It made no sense for him to risk his life and freedom over something so insignificant.

"The report didn't say which person he stole it from," I said. "It didn't say much at all, actually. It was just a load of waffle about magical laws."

"Yes, well," she said. "If there was no doubt that the Seeing Stone had been stolen and he was found with it on his person, the council would have had no choice but to deem him guilty. Especially if he didn't speak out in his own defence."

"The hunters were out to get him from the start," I said. "I don't get it, though. It was my mother who stole the sceptre, right? But by then, she was... dead, and he was on the run. Why would he have then risked his freedom by stealing from the witches? He knew... he must have known he was all I had." I blinked hard, the room wavering before my eyes.

"If he gave a reason, I assume it would have been in the report," she responded. "The Inquisitor wouldn't have been the one who compiled the notes, and all the reports are double-checked for biases. I'm sorry, Blair, but that report is the most accurate account of the trial you're going to find."

Assuming she was right, my dad must have kept his mouth shut about his reasons for stealing the Seeing Stone, even under duress. Yet the hunters had nevertheless seen enough proof to view him as guilty.

"He didn't." I blinked again. "But the hunters were biased against him. It's obvious. My mum ended up dead after she clashed with them and they clearly had a grudge against my dad, too."

And a ghost told me my mother's body disappeared. Did my dad know? Was he on the run the whole time? I could only guess what else had transpired in the years we'd been apart. Even now, I only knew the bare details.

"None of this was widely known, Blair," she said. "All of us assumed your mother had run away, and we'd never met your father."

"Except for the elves," I added. "But I guess they didn't want to intervene in the trial."

The elves kept to themselves, mostly, but they'd come to my dad's aid when he was on the run from the hunters. Before they'd caught him.

"They wouldn't have done," she said. "In a trial which is presided over by the Inquisitor himself, nobody can intervene. The hunters are also well acquainted with dealing with spells and other magical abilities which might influence the outcome of trials, so they'll have accounted for that when they made their decisions."

"I know, but—" I broke off. "Remember Mrs Dailey? And Simeon, when he broke out of jail and hid under an illusion in the courtroom? Witches can have rare abilities, and… and the fairies can use glamour to make anyone see whatever they want to. If that was used in the trial…"

"You'd need proof," she said. "Exact proof from an eyewitness—and even that wouldn't be enough to over-rule the Inquisitor's word."

A lump grew in my throat. "I figured, but I can't let this go."

"Tread carefully, Blair," she said. "I wouldn't advise you to draw unwanted attention after the note the Inquisitor sent you."

"I know," I said. "But this isn't just about me. The Inquisitor's people have always wanted to take over Fairy Falls, regardless of whether I'm here or not. I threw a complication in their way, and so did my dad, but I think this is what the Inquisitor always planned."

"Yes, there are many who would want to overthrow the covens altogether, as Mrs Dailey herself desired," she said. "We don't need to give them an excuse to make a move against us, however."

"That's what Dill wanted," I added. "To remove the witch council so the fairies can come back. He supported the hunters for that reason."

Dill's words echoed in my mind. "*Your people stole our town and drove us out of the magical world at large. The witches collectively drove us away. Just look at this town of yours. Fairy Falls, it's called, and not a single fairy in sight.*"

I didn't know how much truth there was in his words, but he believed the witches had been the ones who'd driven the fairies out of Fairy Falls. He'd been willing to kill for it. It was a well-known fact that fairies had once lived behind the waterfall, but the town's legend said they'd vanished overnight, for no reason anyone had been able to figure out. It'd been centuries ago, and few remembered them ever living here at all. Yet Dill had been certain the witches had been the culprits, and without proof from anyone who'd been alive at the time, I'd had no way to argue against him. In the end, he'd been sent for an extended jail sentence himself for attempted murder and for bewitching my ordinary foster parents in a doomed bid for revenge.

"The fairies," she said. "Perhaps it might be worth pursuing that line of inquiry, Blair, but be careful."

Did she mean to suggest I should ask the fairies myself? That would be a nice idea if I had the faintest idea where to find them. Except for the goblin market, of course, but the market had long since departed. Also, it was difficult to suppress the fear that all the local fairies supported the hunters like Dill did.

"I can ask around, I guess," I said. "Um, have you heard from the Inquisitor since he contacted me?"

Her jaw tensed. "No. If I had, I'd have an idea of how to proceed from here. For now, I'm going to call the former Head Witch and see what she has to say. If she can put me in touch with anyone who served on the regional witch council's committee when your father was arrested, I'll let you know, Blair."

"Thank you," I said. "Um, good luck dealing with her. Sorry I brought this on you."

"Think nothing of it," she said. "I've been wanting a word with her about her neglect to visit her successor."

Um, I'm pretty sure Rebecca has enough problems without the former Head Witch making a reappearance.

I left the office, trying not to feel too annoyed at the regional witch council for letting the hunters arrest my dad without even trying to challenge them. If Madame Grey could find out who'd been involved in his trial, it might help, but the fact remained that the Inquisitor had already got his wish a long time ago. He'd also hidden his fairy nature from everyone else, and hardly anyone knew he was a fairy except for a small group of us, none of whom had any power over him whatsoever.

As for the other fairies? I could only begin to guess if any of them were worth talking to, but they'd left the town centuries ago. Nobody living knew where they'd gone…

I groaned inwardly. Of course there was *one* person in town who'd been alive back then: Vincent the vampire, who happened to be one of the most infuriating people I'd met. He was the person who'd told me about the legend of the fairies' disappearance not long after I'd arrived in town, and if he knew more, you'd think he might have told me at some point, especially if it was relevant to my present dilemma. But Vincent had a tendency to play up to the stereotype of vampires being mysterious and infuriating. Being a mind-reader, he had more of an idea of what went on in my head than most, but that didn't mean he knew the fairies.

Still, someone in town must have a clue where they'd gone, right?

———

When I got home, I grabbed a notepad and began to assemble a list of names of people to speak to.

"You don't have to speak to Vincent," said Alissa, who'd come to help as soon as she realised what I was doing. "You know, even Samuel was alive when your parents were here and he's nowhere near as old as Vincent is."

"He wasn't here when the fairies vanished, though," I said. "How long has he lived in Fairy Falls?"

"Not sure," she said. "I know he came over to England from the Caribbean a few decades ago…"

"That's vampires for you," I said. "I guess I could just ask all of them until someone gives me a straight answer. Wait, wouldn't the local police have been involved in my dad's trial, too?"

"Steve?" said Alissa. "He hasn't been the chief of police for that long, but maybe it's worth asking him. Though he probably wouldn't have known the details of a trial which mostly involved the hunters and the regional witch council."

I added Steve's name to the list. "I know he probably won't talk, especially if I so much as hint that I want to get my dad out of jail. In fact, if I do, he'll give me a shiny new cell of my own."

"You aren't wrong," said Alissa. "I doubt the police will have any new information. If the fairies *and* the witches were involved in the trial, they have countless ways of hiding evidence if they're unscrupulous enough."

"Question was, who did it?" I put the pen down. "Something must have convinced all the members of the regional witch council that my dad was unquestionably guilty. Madame Grey said there were rules against magical interference, but I bet none of them knew the

Inquisitor was a fairy. They might have overlooked something else."

"Well, the obvious choice of culprit is Mrs Dailey," said Alissa. "We already know she had contacts among the hunters *and* the police. And she's a witch. I know she said she didn't belong to a coven, but maybe she pulled some strings with the regional council."

"Wouldn't put it past her," I said. "I asked Rebecca about Blythe, and she said she'd send her sister to talk to me the next time she saw her. It's worth seeing if she remembers anything from the time."

"Never thought I'd see the day she'd help you out," said Alissa. "I wonder where she's living?"

"No idea," I said. "I'm not even sure if she's permanently back in town. I think she's just watching her sister from a distance to make sure nobody takes advantage of her position as Head Witch. Like what happened with those werewolves."

"True," she said. "If you ask me, her mother's more likely to take advantage than most."

"And she has the Pixie-Glass I was looking for at the market." I smothered a sigh. "Why can nothing ever be simple?"

"Because this is the hunters we're talking about," she said. "My grandmother has a point, though. Don't tick off the Inquisitor without definite proof."

"But Mrs Dailey is fair game, on account of her being jailed," I added. "Not that I can stride into the LPFP and ask her, mind. Blythe, though... maybe she can give me some useful information, assuming she's willing to speak to me."

Who else might have been involved, though? Someone

aside from the Inquisitor had seen to it that my dad couldn't plead anything but guilty, but unless I got to speak to him directly, I couldn't piece together all the details. The Inquisitor might well have fabricated the whole trial, of course, but it wasn't out of the realm of possibility that the witches had had a hand in the setup. The person responsible clearly hadn't been a fan of my mother, so Mrs Dailey was the obvious choice. That line of questioning would have to wait until I talked to Blythe, so who else had known her at the time? Madame Grey, Rita… and Veronica. Oh, and old Ava the seer, though half of what she said was cryptic and made little sense. Still, she occasionally came out with some useful advice hidden among her ramblings, when she wasn't pretending to hex the nurses and trying to escape the ward where she lived in the local hospital.

"Ava?" said Alissa, peering at the names on my list. "Have you ever had a coherent conversation with her?"

"She told me to beware of the fairies before I knew they were a threat," I said. "She's also a seer. Isn't that Seeing Stone my father supposedly stole meant to work like a crystal ball?"

"Yeah, but I'm not an expert," she said. "You'd have to ask… I don't know. Who's that new seer in town again?"

"Violet Layne," I said. "I didn't get the impression she knew anything about the fairies…"

"Few people do," she said. "As for who actually stole the Seeing Stone and saw to it that your dad took the blame, I'm not sure there's any way to find out without speaking to any witnesses."

"It was planted on him," I said firmly. "He was framed. I know he was."

"Of course, Blair," she said gently, "but the evidence is stacked against him, and it's been years since the trial."

"Then we'll get to the truth," I said. "I think it's worth talking to Ava, at least."

If nothing else, the Inquisitor would never guess that the elderly witch with a penchant for mischief had known about the fairies' return before anyone else in town.

———

Without further delay, we headed to the local hospital where Alissa worked. Her co-worker, Lou, waved at us when we walked into the waiting room.

"We've come to see old Ava," said Alissa. "Hope that's okay."

"I think Blair sees her more often than her own grand-daughter does," said Lou. "What's it about this time?"

"Seer stuff," I said vaguely. "Things she hinted at that I'd like to know more about."

"You shouldn't humour her," she said. "She predicted we'd all drop dead of the plague last week."

Hmm. Maybe this wasn't such a good idea after all, but I had to at least try out all my options. Ava was probably the least dangerous of all the possible people to question.

"We won't be long," added Alissa. "Blair, go on ahead."

I followed Lou towards the ward for the long-term patients. Ava had been the victim of a backfiring wand accident some years ago and had moved here for her own safety as much as everyone else's. The ward contained an eccentric array of permanent residents, from the man with antlers growing out of his head to a witch whose status as chess champion of the ward remained unmatched.

And then there was Ava, whose escape attempts and tendency to invite people here for private fortune-tellings exasperated the nurses on a daily basis. She wore her usual purple wig, her wand sticking out from behind her ear—not a real wand, as I'd been reassured on more than one occasion—and wore a dress patterned with broomsticks. She didn't seem to notice me until I approached her.

"Hey, Ava." I kept a sensible distance from her in case she started sending hexes in my direction or tried to escape through the door behind me.

"Briar," she said. "Beware the winged one."

"You mean the fairies?" I said, recalling she'd said the exact same line to me at least once before. "Which fairy in particular? Because there's a lot of people I need to beware at the moment, I think."

She chuckled. "Got yourself into trouble, have you, Briar?"

"Blair," I said. "It's Blair."

My mother had originally intended to name me Briar Wildflower, so I supposed Ava must have picked the name up from Tanith, but that didn't mean I wanted the whole ward to know.

"Beware the winged one," she repeated. "I see him, clear as day."

Him. The Inquisitor? I bit my tongue to avoid saying his name aloud. "I think I know who you mean. And yes, I'll beware of him."

"Good," she said. "Beware the liar."

Liar is right. He was fooling everyone in plain sight.

"Um, I had a question I wanted to ask you. Have you ever used a Seeing Stone? It's for seeing into the future, like a crystal ball, right?"

"No," she replied. "Not at all. They aren't for the likes of me. The Seeing Stone contains powerful magic, with no need of a seer to wield it."

A chill raced down my back. "You mean someone who isn't a seer can use it to see the future?"

She inclined her head. "Foolish of them to try. Only a seer can handle knowing what is to come."

"Have you ever heard of someone stealing a Seeing Stone from the region's witch council?" I asked. "About three or four years ago?"

"Yes," she said solemnly. "Yes, I remember it well."

"You do?" I tried to keep the urgency out of my voice, aware that anyone else might be listening in and might repeat my words to the wrong ears. "Did they ever catch who did it? Who was in charge of the trial?"

"Fairies are tricksters," she said. "Beware the liar."

I knew who *that* was. The Inquisitor's entire existence was built on a lie, after all. "Was it a fairy who stole it?"

"Beware, Briar, beware." She repeated the words over and over, and I couldn't get another word of sense out of her. When Lou came into the ward to lead her away, I gave up and left the room in defeat.

Maybe I should speak to the town's other seer after all, though the more people I spoke to, the higher the risk that word would make it back to the hunters. Old Ava was known for talking nonsense and making false predictions, and if she declared to everyone else in the ward that the fairies were coming to take over the town, they'd assume she was talking nonsense. Yet her words had held a current of truth. Not least her comments about the Seeing Stone.

The question was, who had truly been the one to steal it? If not my dad, someone must have framed him, someone who had clout enough to convince the Inquisitor to convict my dad... not that he'd have needed much persuasion, considering his grudge against my family.

I rubbed my forehead. That my dad hadn't deserved his ultimate fate, I had no doubt whatsoever. But could I win in a game of wits against the most powerful hunter in the region?

4

fter I met up with Alissa again in the waiting room, we left the hospital. Lost in thought, I walked out the doors and almost collided with someone I hadn't expected to see for a while.

Blythe stepped out of my way, her usual scowl in place. "Do you ever look where you're going?"

"Whoa," I said. "Sorry."

Alissa shot me a sideways look. "I'll go on ahead, okay, Blair?"

"Sure." I looked at Blythe, and she looked stonily back. Not a friendly expression, though I shouldn't have expected her to be thrilled at the idea of speaking to me again.

"Um, hi, Blythe," I said. "I take it your sister said I wanted to talk to you?"

"What more is there to say?" she asked.

Well... a lot. The last time we'd spoken to one another, she'd relayed her own history with my family. Her mother had constantly railed against mine, feeding her own animosity, but she'd never mentioned my dad. Didn't mean Mrs Dailey hadn't been involved in his capture, though. Blythe herself had been living here in Fairy Falls when my dad had been arrested, come to think of it, and I'd have thought she might have had a passing interest in the case.

"I have some information I didn't have before," I said. "Nathan got me the case files from my dad's arrest."

"You read them?" she said.

"Yes," I said. "The files say he was arrested for stealing a Seeing Stone from the regional witch council, but the reports seem to be missing a bunch of key details about how he was caught, and who was responsible for convicting him. I think you can tell me more."

She arched a brow. "What makes you say that?"

"Your mother," I said. "She hated my family. Did she steal this Seeing Stone and then set my dad up to take the fall?"

"Blunt, much?" she said. "No, she didn't."

I hadn't expected her to have such confidence in her mother's innocence. "How do you know?"

"Because she wasn't in the area at the time," she said. "Besides, my mother wouldn't have stolen anything from the regional council members. You might not believe me, but she wanted to make a bid for a position on the council once herself. She wouldn't have risked getting caught."

I had my doubts. This was Mrs Dailey we were talking about, after all. Blythe wasn't on her mother's side, but that didn't mean she had no blind spots where Mrs Dailey was concerned.

"It was only, what, three or four years ago?" I said.

"According to the elves, anyway. You must remember a trial involving a fairy. They can't be that common, surely."

"The hunters don't make their trials public, and it's not like I kept tabs on them," she said. "As for the regional witch council, none of them live here in Fairy Falls. Ask Madame Grey."

"Already did," I said. "She wasn't involved, either. She said she'd find out more, but at least one witch must have been at the trial who helped ensure that my dad was jailed for life, and I'd like to know who it was."

"Don't look at me," she said. "At the time, nobody knew my connection with your family, and besides, I've never been involved with the hunters."

"Didn't you know about your mother's connections with them, though?" I said. "You must have done."

"I told you, she'd already left town years before your dad's arrest," she said. "I'd moved away from home by then, besides. Why am I wasting my time explaining to you, anyway? I'm not her. I don't want to burn down the covens and let the hunters take their place."

"Or the fairies," I added. "You also knew the secret identity of a certain Inquisitor."

She was silent for a moment, knowing I'd caught her out. It'd been her who'd clued me in to the leader of the hunters being a fairy to begin with. She'd known Buck was one, too.

"My mother told me," she finally said. "She warned me never to cross the Inquisitor and told me he was the most feared person in the region. And she fears nobody."

"Uh-huh," I said. "What about the fact that the hunters have a bunch of other fairies they've personally recruited? Did she tell you that?"

"Mentioned it in passing," she said. "Look, if you want to know why the Inquisitor hated your dad enough to have him framed and arrested, I haven't a clue. I can't say I know who he recruited to help him, but I think his word would have been enough to condemn your dad to a life sentence."

"I didn't think you were involved," I said, "but I'd like to know who stole the Seeing Stone, if the Inquisitor didn't take it himself. Madame Grey's contacting the witches who were on the council at the time, but if you know anything…"

"I don't." She paused. "But I do know the address of someone who knew your parents."

My mouth dropped open. "What? You do? Why didn't you tell me?"

"Because it might not lead to anything." She held out a piece of paper, and I took it from her, reading the name 'Conor Underwood'. "I don't know this person. Never met him. I got the address when I asked around at the goblin market for anyone who knew your dad."

"I take it you mean someone who actually liked him?" I said, recalling Dill, who'd made no secret of how much he hated my dad for choosing to be with my mother.

"Of course," said Blythe. "Or so I heard, anyway."

"Who is this Conor Underwood, then?" I asked. "A witch or a fairy?"

"Find out for yourself," she said. And without another word, she walked away.

"Blunt, much?" I muttered, but she didn't look back.

At least my lie-sensing power hadn't activated at her words, proving she hadn't lied outright to me. The address *did* belong to someone who knew my parents. Or so she believed, anyway. I didn't know why I'd expected her to help me, considering our history of animosity towards one another. Maybe it was our conversation the other week that had made me hope she might be in a more accommodating mood. Her mother was in jail. It wasn't like she could sneak up on the pair of us and bring an army of hunters to arrest us for daring to think of proving my dad's innocence.

Regardless, I was jumpier than usual when I walked home, possibly due to Ava's paranoia rubbing off on me. Yet I couldn't help but feel hopeful about the address I now had in my hands. And despite myself, I trusted that Blythe wouldn't have given it to me if it was a dud. *I think.*

I caught up to Alissa as she was unlocking the front door to our flat.

"How was it?" asked Alissa. "I take it you didn't end up duelling with one another?"

I followed her inside. "Blythe told me she knew absolutely nothing whatsoever, then gave me the address of someone who knew my parents."

"Seriously?" she said. "Who?"

"Someone called Conor Underwood." I held up the scrap of paper. "His address is in Fairy Falls, for what it's worth. She said she got the info from someone at the goblin market, but supposedly this guy actually liked my dad… unlike Dill."

"Are you sure he isn't going to have you arrested on the spot?" asked Alissa. "Or try to put you under a spell, like Dill did?"

"Nope," I said. "I mean, Blythe is the one who gave me the address."

"Yeah, there is that," she said. "Seems fishy. Why didn't

she mention knowing someone who was friends with your parents beforehand?"

"You're forgetting I got her fired from her job, after which she left town, and then I accidentally got her sister promoted to Head Witch?" I said. "She might not hate me anymore, but I don't think she'll ever *like* me. This is a huge favour coming from her."

"You aren't wrong," she said. "So the address is here in Fairy Falls?"

I read the words on the paper. "Looks that way. Whitethorn Street, wherever that is."

"Hmm, that's over by the woods," she said. "Makes sense for a fairy."

"If you say so," I said. "I thought I was the only one."

"Don't forget the goblin market," she said. "Maybe one of their members stayed behind after the others left town."

"I doubt it," I said. "This was someone who was here three or four years ago, when my dad was on the run. Maybe even earlier than that, back when my parents were both alive and living in the same place."

If they ever had. My parents had left me as a baby in the normal world because they'd had no choice in the matter. I'd grown up completely oblivious about my real heritage, and while it would have been tempting to imagine I might have been able to do something about their situation if I'd entered the paranormal world earlier than my mid-twenties, I doubted that was the case. Even now, I wasn't sure I was ready to face up to everything my parents had tried their best to protect me from.

My phone buzzed with a message from Nathan, asking to meet up at the Troll's Tavern. I ducked into my room to change first, swatting the pixie out of my wardrobe and resigning myself to leaving a trail of glitter everywhere again. Tomorrow was Saturday, so I'd pay a visit to this mysterious friend of my family's in the morning. I had a feeling Nathan would want to come with me, but I wasn't sure if that was the right approach. If my dad's friend was a fairy, he must have hidden himself away for a reason, and I'd bet the hunters had been partially responsible. There was no way any fairy still living in the area didn't think of them as a potential threat.

"How was old Ava, anyway?" asked Alissa when I returned to the living room after changing into a fresh outfit.

"Cryptic as ever," I said. "She kept warning me against trusting the fairies, as if I didn't already know it, but she didn't have anything new to say about them. Oh, I asked her about the Seeing Stone, too, and she told me *anyone* can use it to see into the future. Even someone who isn't a witch or a seer."

Her brow wrinkled. "Did she think your dad stole it, then?"

"She stopped making sense at that point." I released a sigh. "So I'll have to wait for Madame Grey's update. I thought about checking in with Violet Layne as well. She's the only other seer in town, and she probably knows all about the Seeing Stone, too."

"Yeah, she might," she said. "It's more of a ceremonial item, though, according to my grandmother. Seeing Stones are rarely used by actual seers. I think they're even rarer than Pixie-Glasses, from what I've heard."

The doorbell rang. Nathan was here. I walked to the door, and Sky headbutted the back of my leg. "What?"

"Miaow," he said.

"Miaow yourself." He padded after me to the doorstep and greeted Nathan by rubbing against his ankles. Nathan himself looked a little startled. The little cat was notoriously fickle with his affections and while he liked attention, he tended to prefer it from me above anyone else. Unlike a regular witch familiar, he was a fairy cat and therefore not bound to me like a regular familiar, but we'd chosen one another, for what it was worth. Just like Nathan and I had chosen one another, too.

Everything in my new life had been the same: a choice. Even accepting the invitation to come to Fairy Falls, since Veronica hadn't known who I was when she'd offered me the job at Dritch & Co. The decision had been up to me, and right now, I stood at another crossroads. If I visited this Connor Underwood person, I knew in my heart there would be no turning back.

Before we left for the pub, I told Nathan about my conversation with Blythe. He reacted in the exact way I'd expected: with suspicion.

"Who is this Conor Underwood person?" he asked. "I didn't know there were any fairies living here."

"I'm not sure what kind of fairy he is," I admitted. "Blythe said she'd never met him in person. She got the address from the market."

"Then I don't think you should go alone," he said. "Don't get me wrong, I'm sure she's probably not out to get you…"

"This time," I added. "The thing is, I'm not sure he'd want to talk to me with anyone else there. If he's a fairy, then I think I have to do this on my own."

"MIAOW," said Sky.

I turned to the little fairy cat. "You want to come with me?"

Nathan nodded. "Sky will keep you safe, I'm sure."

"Miaow," Sky agreed.

My heart lifted. Sky had chosen me, too. First when he'd chosen me as his witch, or fairy, but now he'd chosen to face my history at my side.

We'd stand by one another, whatever came our way. I might not know if my choice was the right one, but I wasn't alone.

———

I set off for Conor Underwood's house early the following morning. Mist curled over the hilltops and brushed the tips of the trees, while the distant crash of the waterfall filled the air. Sky padded alongside me, occasionally overtaking me and waiting for me to catch up.

Nathan texted me telling me to let him know how it went, and to check in with him immediately after I'd spoken to Conor. He respected my desire to go alone, but that didn't keep him from worrying. I didn't mind. If our positions were reversed, I'd be worried, too.

I debated whether to get my wings out or not as I walked, but every time I stalled, Sky meowed loudly as though to discourage me from turning back. Hardly anyone was out at this time in the morning, so I used my Seven-Millimetre Boots to skim through the centre of Fairy Falls towards the wilder areas near the town's boundary. The sound of the waterfall grew louder as we reached the spot where the town merged with the forest.

As I'd suspected, finding the right street was difficult.

It took me a long time before I found a patch of trees near the road and a crooked sign saying, 'Whitethorn Street', but the road didn't even go in a straight line. Then the numbers stopped as the road dead-ended against a patch of trees. I couldn't see a way around it, so I wove through the trees and found the road continued along a winding track which seemed more forest than road. The rest of the town had disappeared from sight beyond a wall of trees, and I walked until I came to a cottage standing in a wild, overgrown garden. The place had a storybook feel, with whitewashed walls covered in twisting vines and a red tiled roof. Vibrant shades of flowers filled the rest of the space, bringing a fragrant scent. My senses kicked into overdrive.

I checked the number on the door. This was the place.

Drawing in a breath, I walked up to the red-painted door and knocked. Nobody answered at first, while I hovered awkwardly on the spot, realising I didn't have a clue if Conor Underwood actually knew who I was or not. Which of my parents had he known? Based on the fairylike atmosphere of the place, it was more likely to be my dad, but I felt more of a clumsy human than a witch at the moment and even less like a fairy.

I knocked again. The door opened, and a fairy stood on the other side.

5

____

While my paranormal senses instantly registered him as a fairy, the man was glamoured to look human. His hair was faintly blond, his face pointed, but strangely inhuman in a way I couldn't quite put my finger on. I blinked, willing myself to see past his façade, and a bright sheen covered my vision and revealed the wings sprouting from his shoulders. We looked at one another for a long moment. Then Sky meowed loudly, breaking the silence.

"Hey," I said. "I'm Blair Wilkes. I don't know if you've heard about me, but someone gave me your address and said you knew my parents."

The fairy gave me a long look. "I am Conor Underwood."

"Um, nice to meet you." A thousand questions came to mind, and I struggled to sort through them all. "Did you really know my parents? My dad—Braden Eventide? Or Tanith Wildflower, my mother?"

"I knew your father, Blair," he said. "I also knew of

your mother, though she died before I could ever meet her."

"You knew my dad," I said. "But... I've never heard of you before."

"I didn't know he had a child," he said. "A half fairy, half witch child. Interesting."

He was looking at me as though I was a specimen in a cage. It made me slightly uncomfortable, to say the least.

"Why?" I said. "Why are you here? I thought there weren't any fairies left in the town at all."

"We hide in the cracks of the world," he said. "I thought you knew."

I shook my head. "I'm not sure I understand what that means."

"You're too human."

His words needled me. "That's hardly my fault. I grew up human—normal, even. My parents wanted to keep me safe, and they didn't have a choice. I'm trying to learn how to be a fairy, but it's difficult when you're so hard to find. Where have you been hiding all this time?"

"I did not mean to offend you," he said. "However, you must know you're no longer where you thought you were."

He pointed over my shoulder. I turned on the spot and stifled a gasp. There were no signs of the rest of Fairy Falls whatsoever. Just a forest, bathed in sunlight. In fact, there wasn't a single cloud in the sky, even though it'd been a gloomy, overcast day when I'd walked here. It was as though I'd stepped through a portal into another world. I looked down at my feet and screwed up my eyes against the brightness of the grass. Then it hit me that at some point I'd ended up floating above the ground. My wings had come out without my even noticing.

I looked at Conor. "How is this possible? Where *are* we?"

"If anyone else had gone looking for my address, they wouldn't have found me," he said. "But you did."

"How…" The words escaped me for a moment. "How long have you been here?"

"A while," he said. "Long enough to have known your father. We came to know one another quite well, in fact, but he moved on, and I haven't seen him in years."

"But—you must know he was jailed, right?" I said. "He was locked up for life in the Lancashire Prison for Paranormals."

How could he not know? I could hardly believe he'd been hidden in plain sight all this time, for that matter, but it seemed the fairies had never left at all. In spite of my shock, hope spread inside my chest at the notion that against all the odds, I'd found another fairy after all.

On the other hand, I couldn't let myself forget Dill. *He'd* known my dad, too, yet he'd hated him for choosing to be loyal to my mother rather than the other fairies. He'd believed the witches had driven the fairies out of Fairy Falls and he'd chosen to side with the hunters in the hopes that they'd allow the fairies to displace the covens. For all I knew, maybe Conor Underwood thought the same. I didn't know him, not really, and trusting him might break my heart all over again.

"I know he is," he said. "His capture is why it took me so long to realise you were his daughter. However, there is nothing I could have done to prevent them from taking him. Exiled fairies hold a far lower status than ones who belong to the Courts, and I was exiled from among the Court fairies a long time ago."

"Oh," I said. "I'm sorry. But… what is a Court, exactly? Like, a kingdom or something? Or a town?"

"Of a sort," he said. "There are many different Courts which are as varied as your human communities. Personally, I found it stifling to belong to a Court, so I left mine a long while ago. Nevertheless, your father was welcoming to me. Somewhat surprising, given his status."

I frowned. "What do you mean, status? I thought… I mean, he lived among humans, not fairies. He wouldn't have met my mother otherwise."

"Perhaps he did," he said, "But I knew him as Braden Eventide, Prince of the Court of Eventide."

His words reverberated around my mind for a long moment as shock and disbelief flooded me. "*A prince? How is that possible?*"

This couldn't be real. My dad would have told me, surely.

"*Yes, a prince who was in* voluntary exile," he said. "Now I know he had a child, I understand why he left his Court."

My mind felt stuck, frozen in shock. "Did my mum know? She must have."

"There are more fairy princes than there are human ones," he said. "It's by no means a rarity among our kind."

"Still." I sought to get a handle on the flood of questions swirling in my head. "Does that mean… he was the heir to his Court? If he wasn't in jail, would he have to go back?"

"No," he said. "He chose to exile himself and with good reason. If the others found out he had a human child, I doubt they would have looked favourably on him. Especially a child of a witch."

"But—" I broke off. "The paranormal hunters arrested my dad and locked him up. How could they accuse a *prince* of committing a crime? Wouldn't the rest of his family been able to stop them from arresting him?"

"You're thinking in a human way," he said. "Most fairies are loyal to their own Courts and consider that a higher priority than family. Since your father abandoned his fellow fairies, they would have left him to his fate."

His words rang in my skull, impossible and yet unarguable. My dad was a *prince. If the fairies had seen him as having betrayed them by leaving, it explained why none of them had leapt to his defence against the hunters, but I couldn't help wondering why this fairy hadn't intervened. Instead, he'd stayed hidden in this idyllic bubble, cut off from the outside world.*

"Does anyone from Fairy Falls know you live here?" I asked. "Any other humans, I mean? Madame Grey, or the witches?"

A flash of some emotion crossed his face. "No."

"Or the elves?" I pressed.

"Why would I tell *them?*" he asked.

"Ah… the elves met my dad, too," I explained. "The elf king knew the fairies hadn't left this world entirely and they predicted your return before almost anyone else did."

"I never left, Blair," he said. "Whatever the witches may claim."

"Is it just you?" I couldn't help asking. "I mean, are there others?"

"Other fairies in exile?" he said. "Of course. I, however, keep to myself, and it's been a long while since I've seen any of them."

"You saw my dad, though," I said. "Are you sure he never mentioned the hunters to you? Because they're recruiting fairies to work for them. They've been targeting half-fairies who live among humans, anyway. Has that always been the case?"

His jaw tensed. "Not to my knowledge."

I thought not. Fairies were different even by paranormal standards, and the notion of any of them joining the hunters had always struck me as discordant even after learning their leader's true nature. The hunters attracted the sort of people who'd think nothing of shooting a werewolf who stepped out of line or locking up an innocent man for a crime he'd never committed. Paranormal communities were close-knit, despite their differences, and it had never made sense to me that they would readily turn on their own.

The Inquisitor, though, had made a career out of pretending to be human. Even to the other fairies he recruited. Perhaps, like Buck, they were unaware of any alternative. Regardless of how and why they'd made the choice to join him, however, the Inquisitor still had more fairies on his team than I did. Conor had been polite enough so far, but that didn't mean he'd be willing to take a stand against the hunters. Given that he'd been hiding out here for years, he didn't strike me as the confrontational type. Besides, for all I knew, he was reporting directly to the hunters himself. I couldn't discount the possibility, not after the last fairy I'd met had turned out to be anything but an ally.

I fidgeted, trying to remember what else I'd planned to ask him. "I wondered... do you know whereabouts I might be able to learn more about using fairy magic? Is glamour all there is to it?"

He gave me a strange look. "Glamour is everything, and everything you see before you is made from glamour."

I looked up at the bright sky, the trees, the vibrant garden, and then back at the cottage and its owner. Then it hit me that someone was missing.

"Where's Sky?" I asked. "Um, my fairy cat?"

"You have a fairy cat?" he said. "I didn't know they consented to being pets."

"He adopted me, not the other way around," I said. "Might he have got lost somewhere in the forest?"

How big was this weird bubble universe, anyway? If it was all made out of pure glamour, then it might go on forever for all I knew. When the fairy didn't answer, I turned away from the house and surveyed the garden. "Sky?"

"MIAOW." His voice came from somewhere in the bushes.

I trod between the clouds of wildflowers and found Sky entangled in the tendrils of a giant plant. He hissed and lashed out with his claws, unable to free himself from the grasping vines.

I grabbed my wand and cast a harmless shielding spell, but if anything, that enraged the plant more. Several thorny tendrils shot in my direction, and I beat my wings, hovering off the ground in an attempt to avoid getting speared.

Sky growled, then turned into his giant monster form. The plant's grip on him broke, and he leapt for freedom. In one bound, he shot past me and out of the garden into the forest.

"Sky!" I stumbled out of the plants and reached the

doorstep where Conor stood. "I have to go after him, but I want to ask you something first."

"Yes?" The fairy showed not a hint of concern that his plants had attacked me.

"I wanted to know how the hunters came to be under the control of the fairies," I said. "I know you've been out of touch for a while, but you know something, don't you? Why do they have it in for my family?"

He was silent for a moment. "I've been absent from the magical world for a long time, Blair, but many of my fellow fairies have never forgiven the witches for what they did to us. Perhaps therein lies the answer, but the only way for you to know for certain is to ask them directly."

I hesitated, wanting to ask more, but Sky's absence worried me more than my need for answers. "Okay. Thanks. I… I'll come back."

As he withdrew into the house, I crossed the garden and found the little cat sulking outside the gate. Crouching beside him, I gave him a stroke. "You all right?"

"Miaow," he grumbled.

I stroked him again, wishing I could reassure myself as easily. I'd learned more than I'd ever expected to from Conor, but even he hadn't been able to tell me how the hunters had come to be under control of the fairies. Even most of the hunters themselves didn't even know their leader was a paranormal masquerading as a regular human, and it wasn't like I had contact with any of them regardless. Except…

Nathan's family. Mr Harker had held the details of my dad's trial. He *must* have some idea of what the Inquisitor had done to manipulate my dad's arrest, even if the

Inquisitor was fooling him as much as anyone else. He and I were long overdue a conversation, as we hadn't spoken since before the Inquisitor had made his recent offer to me.

And he'll happily hand over the Pixie-Glass, will he? He'd pretty much told me I didn't deserve to be part of the paranormal world at all. Yet it seemed his old boss didn't agree, because the Inquisitor *did* want to hire me to work for the hunters, despite my dad's imprisonment. I was enough of a potential asset that he didn't care about my family's supposed criminal dealings.

Mr Harker, on the other hand, was a rule-follower. The Inquisitor *made* the rules, and his manipulative nature explained why he and Blythe's mother got on so well. Yet I didn't have direct contact with him the way I did with Nathan's family. His dad and brothers hadn't exactly taken to me the last time we'd seen one another, but they might not necessarily be aware that the Inquisitor had tried to hire me. If I told Mr Harker, he might drop his guard and let something slip about my dad's arrest. Or I might be able to sew a thread of doubt about his former boss's integrity. It was worth a shot.

With Sky at my side, I walked through the strange illusory forest and retraced my steps away from the cottage. As I did so, the brightness faded to the overcast sky peeking through a canopy of branches. I'd made it back into the real world. I halted for a moment, turning on my heel to look behind me, but the bright forest had vanished as if it had never existed.

I also didn't recognise my surroundings. Oh, no. *Please say I'm at least near Fairy Falls.* I didn't need to spend the rest of the day lost in the extensive forest which covered the upper side of the lake.

"Sky, do you know the way out?" I said hopefully.

"Miaow," he said, and stepped ahead of me onto the path.

We walked in silence for a few minutes, but the end of the forest didn't grow any closer, nor did we appear to be anywhere near Whitethorn Street. The house was well-hidden, I'd say that much. Were there other fairies hiding in plain sight, too? Why were they afraid to show their faces? *He mentioned the witches. Do they all truly blame the witches of Fairy Falls for their exile?*

I spotted a small figure ahead of me, an elf with twig-coloured clothing and small limbs. I knew him. He was named Bramble, and he worked for the king.

"Blair Wilkes," he said. "What are you doing here?"

"I'm lost," I admitted. "I think I was just in fairyland a minute ago, and when I left, I ended up here."

"You were with one of *them?*" he growled. "Be careful, Blair."

Everyone seems to be saying that to me lately. The problem was that there was no safe path no matter what choice I made. Even if I opted against directly contacting the Inquisitor, he might well show up to recruit me in person anyway. Yet giving up on my dad was out of the question, even if it meant risking being bedazzled by a fairy once again.

"I didn't know there were fairies in hiding near Fairy Falls," I said pointedly, wondering how much the elf knew of our hidden neighbours. "I thought they all left."

"Most did," he said. "Those who stayed behind don't interact with the rest of us, for the most part."

I figured as much. He didn't seem keen on the elves. "What did the witches do that made the fairies hate them so much?"

"The witches take what isn't theirs," growled Bramble. "As the hunters do."

"I'm pretty sure the local witches have never locked up an innocent man on false charges," I said. "Madame Grey is a good person."

Besides, it was the *fairies* the hunters had tried to recruit.

"She might be," he said, "but others are not."

I decided not to argue. The elves had an ongoing feud with the witches over their territory in the forest. Most of the witches I'd met had been nothing but kind to me, but I'd also met witches who schemed to get what they wanted, too. Mrs Dailey being a prime example. And most of the fairies had gone into hiding for a good reason. Even from the elves.

Come to think about it, my dad's status as a prince explained why the Elf King had allowed him to hide in the forest when he'd been on the run from the hunters. I'd bet he'd told the Elf King his real identity, yet none of them had let a word slip to me.

Not that being a prince had helped him avoid getting caught by the hunters in the end.

"Maybe, but the hunters are run by one of the fairies," I said to the elf. "I can't seem to avoid them."

"Then try not to get killed," he said. "My king would prefer it if you lived. We need the hunters to stay out of our forest, and so far, you're the only person who's succeeded in driving them off."

I doubt I could keep the Inquisitor away if he wanted your territory. I decided not to argue the point, though. I had an inkling the elves would end up disappointed if they expected me to effectively defend them against the hunters, but I wasn't about to complain about having someone else on my team. They'd helped my dad hide from the hunters, after all, which was more than most people had done.

"I'll try my best not to, but it'd help if you could point me to the way out of the forest," I said.

The elf did so, and Sky padded on ahead, with a flick of his tail and a *miaow* which seemed to say, *I already knew the way out.*

As I walked, my phone buzzed with a message from Nathan, a reminder that at least one person unquestionably had my back. Might Nathan's father have more to say about my dad's trial? It was safe to say he would not support my idea of proving my dad's innocence, but it was worth speaking to Nathan's family myself. Maybe they'd be more willing to listen to me than the Inquisitor.

6

————————

After I'd left the forest, I went to meet Nathan. His text had been sent several minutes ago, while I'd been lost in the woods, so I sent him a response reassuring him that I was okay. Sky padded ahead of me down the road lined with terraced houses, which appeared positively ordinary compared to the otherworldly place I'd just been to. Murderous garden aside, I understood the appeal of using glamour to create a nice place to live, but living in there alone for years without ever interacting with anyone else struck me as a bit excessive.

I snapped my fingers to put away my fairy wings, then I knocked on the door to Nathan's house. He answered a moment later. "Oh, hey, Blair."

I thought he sounded slightly edgier than usual… then I noticed he wasn't alone. Someone else lurked in the hall-way: Eric, Nathan's younger brother and Erin's twin. I found myself doubly glad I'd put away my wings. From Nathan's expression, this was not a planned visit. I'd wanted to talk to his family, but not immediately after Conor's revelations had shaken me to the core.

I realised I'd been staring at Eric for the last few seconds and managed to close my mouth. "Um. Hello, Eric."

"Blair," he said. "You're still here?"

"Yes," I said. "Where else would I be?"

"That's enough, Eric," Nathan said sharply. "Of course Blair's still here."

Oh, very funny. It seemed Eric agreed with his father that I didn't belong in the paranormal world at all. Which, I wouldn't deny, still stung a little, even though Nathan unequivocally disagreed with his brother. So did Erin. Did she know her twin brother was in town?

"Miaow," said Sky loudly, as if to say, *I'm here, too.*

I closed the door behind me, not wanting the whole street to witness the fallout if my cat decided to retaliate against Eric's unfriendliness. Given that the first time I'd met Nathan's family, I'd wrecked their family dinner by accidentally inviting a troop of elves and a pixie into the house, it came as no surprise that they hadn't warmed to me by now. My cat hadn't exactly helped matters by inviting himself for a visit at the same time, either.

Eric scowled at his brother. "You know what Dad said."

"Have I ever given you a reason to assume that I care what he says?" said Nathan.

Eric's jaw twitched. "No, but you went to visit him the other day. I thought the two of you had made it up. You can't walk away from your own family, Nathan. We need you."

I had an inkling I'd interrupted a conversation I wasn't

supposed to be privy to, yet it wasn't my fault Eric had shown up unannounced. It didn't look as though their father had joined him, but the odds of convincing Nathan's scowling, unfriendly younger brother to loan me the Pixie-Glass were almost as low as getting his father to assist me in contacting my dad. In their eyes, he was a criminal and I wasn't much better.

"Being family doesn't give you the right to tell Nathan what to do," I told Eric. "What are you doing here, anyway? Did you walk all the way to Fairy Falls just to berate Nathan?"

He blinked, as though startled to hear my tone. Maybe I'd been sharper than I'd normally be, but after the bombshell Conor had dropped on my head about my own family, I had zero energy left to deal with any more drama. I wanted to talk to my boyfriend. Alone.

On the other hand, I had an opportunity here.

"I came here to talk some sense into my brother, but it's clear you still have him under your spell." Eric walked past me through the hallway.

"Actually, I wanted to speak to your dad myself." I stepped into his path before he reached the door. "About my father's arrest."

"Your criminal father?" he said. "Been in touch with him, have you?"

"Not exactly," I said, wondering if he'd really expected me to admit it if I had. "But I've met a friend of his, and he had some interesting things to say about the hunters' involvement in his capture. With the fairies in general, in fact."

Eric's brows rose, and Nathan shot me a worried look. "What *interesting things* would they be?"

Did he know the Inquisitor was a fairy? I assumed he didn't, but his father might. It didn't make much of a difference either way, really. The Inquisitor was the one who held the keys to my dad's cell… but Nathan's family had the Pixie-Glass. How could I find out its location without giving away my plan?

"Ask your father," I said to him. "If he's willing to tell you the truth, that is."

Nathan's expression flickered with worry, and he started to speak. A knock on the door from behind me interrupted him. I crossed my fingers behind my back that it wasn't the elves come to drag me to see their king. Or the pixie again. *Please not the pixie again.* It was a mercy that Sky was behaving himself… though admittedly, I was the one who'd pushed Eric's buttons. I moved to the door and peered through the spy hole. To my relief, Erin stood on the other side, so I opened the door.

"What're you doing here?" Erin eyed her twin brother with a mixture of confusion and hostility as he walked towards her.

"Talking some sense into Nathan," Eric responded. "Maybe I'll have more luck with you."

"I doubt it," said Erin. "Everyone here knows you're a—"

"MIAOW," said Sky loudly, poking Eric in the ankle. I looked down at the little cat, wondering if Eric had trodden on his paw or something.

"What's his problem?" Eric wanted to know.

"If you kicked my cat—" I began heatedly.

Sky grew to his monster-sized self, dwarfing Nathan's brother. Eric jumped back and dug into his pocket, pulling out a gun.

"No weapons in the house!" said Nathan. "I thought I told you not to carry that thing around Fairy Falls. What if the werewolves had caught you?"

"I think that's what was bothering him," I added, as Sky hissed loudly.

Eric shot me a glare. "I can carry a weapon to protect myself if I want—"

Sky swatted the gun out of his hand with a paw, then gave another hiss.

Erin burst out laughing. "I'm with the cat. What did you expect to have to protect yourself against out here, us?"

Nathan walked over to Sky and looked into his monstrous face. "Can you not do that in the house? It's frightening my brother, and he does foolish things when he's scared."

"Miaow." To my surprise, Sky obeyed and shrank back to his usual size, leaving the gun discarded on the floor.

I cleared my throat. "Sky had a traumatic experience with a plant this morning. He's a bit jumpy."

Now everyone was looking at me as though I'd got my wings out in public, which really wasn't what I needed at this point. I scooped up Sky in my arms, and thankfully, he didn't fight me.

Eric retrieved the gun, then when Sky gave another loud hiss, he stuck it back into his pocket and scowled. "Can't you control that animal?"

"You aren't helping," said Erin. "Shut up, Eric, before you end up clawed to death by Blair's pet monster cat."

I debated telling them it was a glamour and Sky's normal size was the one I held in my arms, but he'd probably give me a poke with his claws if I did. On the other hand, I really did need to talk to the Harker siblings' father, and it wouldn't help my case if my cat terrorised Eric into running off.

I adjusted my grip on Sky. "He's a fairy cat, not a wild animal, and he's more of a housemate than a pet. Anyway, if you could let your dad know I'd like to talk to him, it'd be appreciated."

"Wait, what?" said Erin. "What did I interrupt?"

"Nothing," said Eric. "Nothing that's of any concern to you, anyway."

"We were talking about my dad," I told Erin.

Her eyes rounded. "What about him? Is he still in jail?"

"Of course he is," said Eric. "I suppose I can't be surprised at you for turning out to have similar criminal tendencies, Blair, considering the company you keep."

"What does that mean?" I asked. "I'm with *you* now, technically."

Erin snorted. "She's right, you know."

"I meant that you work for Veronica Eldritch," he said, ignoring his sister. "She spent some time in our prison, too."

For the second time that day, my mouth dropped open as my mind went into freefall. My truth-sensing powers didn't react, which told me he was being honest. My boss had been arrested by the hunters? Since when? "I didn't know anything about that."

"I can't imagine she'd want her employees to know," he said. "Frankly, I'm surprised anyone would want to work with her after that, but she's always had a contentious relationship with the regional witch council, and that Madame Grey is known for giving people second chances even if they don't deserve them."

"Excuse me?" I said. "What does the regional witch council have to do with the hunters?"

The same people who the Seeing Stone belonged to. Had they got Veronica arrested as well? Whether they had or not, this was news to me.

"We have an agreement, of course," he said. "Meaning, the regional witch council gives us permission to punish those who break certain laws. That was the case with Veronica, at least, though she wriggled out of a longer sentence."

"What did she do?" I said. "It can't have been that serious, if you let her go."

"I had nothing to do with the council's decision," he responded. "That honour went to the prosecutor, who claimed her stealing the Seeing Stone was a first offence, and since she didn't do any harm with it, she'd be spared a harsh sentence."

Stealing the Seeing Stone? His words echoed in my ears, yet my lie-sensing power remained dormant. *Veronica* had taken the Seeing Stone? Did he know my dad had been arrested for the same reason? Maybe he did, yet Veronica hadn't been jailed for life the way he had. The person who'd convicted her hadn't been biased against her the way the council had against my dad.

"Who told you that?" I whispered. "The Inquisitor, by any chance?"

"What in the world is a Seeing Stone?" Erin wanted to know.

"A magical device that belongs to the witch covens," said Eric.

"Since when did you know anything about witches?" said Erin. "The last time we talked, you didn't even know the name of the person in charge of this town's leading coven."

Eric shot her a disgruntled look. "Actually, I have a directive to negotiate with the regional witch council on the orders of the Inquisitor himself, as of this week. In fact, I'm his special ambassador."

"You're what?" Why would the Inquisitor need an ambassador to deal with the witches? I'd thought he frequently spoke to them himself. "Have you come to see Madame Grey?"

"No, I've come to convince my brother to stop neglecting his responsibilities and lend his assistance to his family," he said. "I have a meeting with the regional witch council next week, and I'll be representing the Inquisitor himself."

"And you're worried that we'll show you up?" Erin snorted. "We wouldn't have known you had this super-secret job if you hadn't just told us."

The regional witch council. I still had yet to find out who among them had seen to my dad's jail sentence, but that the Inquisitor had sent one of Nathan's brothers to represent him couldn't be a good thing.

They own the Seeing Stone... so at least one of them was involved in jailing my dad.

"Blair will know," Eric said. "As her friend the Head Witch will also be invited to the meeting."

Oh, no. At least the Inquisitor himself wouldn't be there, but Blythe had expected the hunters to take advantage of Rebecca's new position and now would be the perfect time for them to show their hand. And so would any of the witches who secretly supported the hunters' agenda.

"Why do they need the Inquisitor represented at their meeting?" I said. "He's not part of a coven, is he?"

"The hunters are required to be there to keep the witches in line, of course," he said. "We have many witches who support our cause, but we felt it necessary to send an impartial observer."

Erin gave another loud snort. "You sound like you're parroting the Inquisitor. Did he teach you that speech or did you have to practise in front of a mirror?"

"Erin," said Nathan warningly. "What do you mean by 'support our cause'?"

I faced Eric, wanting to know the answer, too.

"That's none of your concern," he said. "The Head Witch is a child, isn't she? I'd have thought Madame Grey would have been careful not to involve her in such matters, but she must be confident in her ability to resist manipulation."

"What, by the Inquisitor?" I said. "Her own *mother* manipulated her talents before she became Head Witch. In fact, Mrs Dailey was a strong supporter of the hunters, yet she's now serving a long sentence in jail. That doesn't say much for the company you keep."

"Jailed or not, she knows her own daughter best." He gave me a withering look. "She seems to know a lot about you, too."

"You *talked* to her?" Mrs Dailey was supposed to be under the highest security possible. "How?"

"Certain prisoners are allowed privileges, if they behave themselves."

A likely story. It seemed the Inquisitor hadn't abandoned her to a life sentence after all… and if Mrs Dailey had the Pixie-Glass with her, she did have a way to communicate with the outside world.

But if that was the case, was it *Eric* who had the other one? Was that why Nathan hadn't been able to find it?

Nathan met my eyes, clearly thinking the same. "Eric, be careful with the Inquisitor."

"I don't need to listen to *you,* Nathan," Eric said. "Let me know if you change your mind."

And without another word, Eric walked out of the house and past his twin sister, one hand on the gun in his pocket.

Erin watched him go, one eyebrow raised. "Wow. Guess that's why he's been acting all high and mighty lately, if the Inquisitor has him acting as a special ambassador."

"And having conversations with high security prisoners?" I added. "How is that even allowed?"

"It shouldn't be," she said. "I know the Inquisitor calls the shots, but even the other hunters would object if he starts giving Mrs Dailey more freedom than she deserves."

"She might not necessarily have left her cell, though," I said. "Not if she has what I think she does."

"Come again?" said Erin.

"The Pixie-Glass," I said. "I think Eric has the other one. That's why it wasn't at your dad's house."

"I knew there was a reason you went home," Erin said to her brother. "What, were you trying to steal it?"

"Borrow," said Nathan. "I have an inkling Eric will say no if I ask him. Now he's working with the Inquisitor directly, it'll be even harder to outwit him."

"I know." I'd dealt with enough shocking revelations

today that discovering Eric had the Pixie-Glass hadn't taken me particularly by surprise, but it'd thrown another wrench in our plans. "I also know that the Inquisitor is trying to get to me. That's why he recruited your brother, I bet, and he's going to keep trying to win my allies over to his side. Starting with the regional witch council, I don't doubt."

"That doesn't mean you need to tick him off more than you have to," he said. "Is it absolutely imperative that you speak to your father?"

"It is," I said, "because he'll be able to fill in the gaps of what I already know. He can tell me the names of everyone involved in his trial and who convicted him, and we can figure out a strategy to expose their lies. If everyone involved had a personal bias against him or obeyed the Inquisitor out of loyalty to him rather than the law, then that's hardly fair."

Erin cleared her throat. "Um, Blair, not that I'm opposed, but... are you sure the Inquisitor won't figure out what you're doing? I mean, he has Eric hanging onto his every word, and my brother's as thick as a block of concrete, so he won't know if the Inquisitor only chose him as his ambassador in order to get at you."

"You aren't wrong," said Nathan. "Blair—"

"Please don't tell me to be careful," I said. "I've had a day of it already. I'll have a think about how I might get the Pixie-Glass from your brother, but I really meant it when I said I'd like to talk to your dad. I'm sure he knows more about the case. And then there's my boss, too..."

"Come again?" said Erin.

"Your brother just said my boss was arrested for the same crime as my dad," I said. "Yet Veronica wasn't punished with a lifelong jail sentence, which makes her proof of their bias. If I can get her to speak out against the hunters…"

"To whom?" Nathan said. "They're the highest authority in the region."

"Aside from the Head Witch," I said. "Rebecca might be a kid, but they still invited her to the regional witch council's meeting. It's required by law. If I ask her to use her authority to back up my word, they'll have to at least listen to my pleas."

"Your father did break the law," he said. "I know the Inquisitor had an agenda, but the fact remains that your dad was convicted and even the Head Witch can't overturn his sentence."

"I know." Frustration burned away my triumph. "But there must be a way. The Inquisitor doesn't hold all the power, even if he thinks he does. Some of the other witches might be willing to stand up to him if I can get them to see that my dad was unlawfully punished."

The truth lay with the fairies, I was sure. If I talked to Conor Underwood again, he might give me an idea of how to contact the others, but given his enmity with the witch covens, perhaps that was wishful thinking on my part.

"Okay, talk to your boss," said Erin. "Veronica, right? She must have been arrested before I joined up with the hunters, because I don't remember them bringing her in."

"Nor me," said Nathan, "but I don't think her word would be enough to get the hunters to admit to inflicting a punishment that was too severe."

"Worth a shot," I said. "I'll get the Pixie-Glass, then I can talk to my dad, and maybe Blythe's mother, too—"

"Absolutely not," Nathan interjected. "She might be in jail, but she's certainly still scheming."

"Your brother has spoken to her recently," I reminded him. "He's getting information directly from her. Why else would he bring up my boss being jailed, too?"

"Blair, you have quite enough enemies already," he said.

"Whoa," said Erin. "You're both stressed. Just chill."

I caught my breath, feeling bad for snapping at Nathan. This was the closest to an argument we'd come in a long time, but the frustration was getting to both of us. Especially with his family involved. I should have known the Inquisitor would exploit his lingering connection to the hunters, but now it seemed more apparent than ever that we were going to have to go against his family in order to save mine.

"Whereabouts is he living?" I willed my tone to stay calm. "Your brother, I mean."

"You mean Eric?" said Erin. "If not with our dad or at the hunters' local base, then I don't know. Maybe he got a new place. I can track him down, no problem."

"Be careful," said Nathan. "If the Inquisitor has singled out our brother, he did it for a reason."

"To keep an eye on the rest of us," said Erin. "I know, I know. Anyway, did you say you got attacked by a plant, Blair?"

"I went to see a fairy this morning," I said. "Let's say I got more than I bargained for."

I gave them a rundown of my conversation with Conor Underwood earlier that day. While I'd planned to talk to Nathan alone, I didn't mind telling Erin. She'd become my friend, and her comments to Eric that morning had cemented my trust that she wouldn't sell me out to her family. If anything, Erin was more shocked than I had been at the fairy's revelation about my dad's real identity.

"Your dad's a *prince?*" she said.

"Apparently," I said. "If you ask me, that seems a major argument for getting his case looked at again. He and the Inquisitor clearly had some kind of long-standing grudge against one another, which shouldn't be enough reason to jail someone for life."

"Nobody aside from us knows the Inquisitor is a fairy," said Nathan. "Not even the hunters. My father doesn't either. He'd never believe me if I told him."

"Then we'll expose him," I said, inspiration striking. "I think that should be our angle. If we reveal the Inquisitor has been lying about being a fairy, *and* that he was the one who ordered my dad's arrest... but we'd have to do it in front of someone who can overrule him."

"Does such a person exist?" said Erin. "Don't get me wrong, I'd like to expose his lies for the world to see, but he's the highest authority in the region and the other hunters in positions of power won't exactly be falling over themselves to get their boss exposed as a fraud. Especially if he's as powerful as you say."

"There can't be nobody who can stand up to him," I said. "What about the witch covens? And the Head Witch and the others? If we got all of them involved in a public exposure... would that work?"

"Maybe," said Erin. "That sounds wildly risky. I'm in."

Nathan frowned. "The Inquisitor is playing games with us. Until we find out why he's chosen Eric as his ambassador and entrusted him with the Pixie-Glass, we shouldn't challenge him directly."

"I know," I said. "But now we have a starting point."

All we had to do now was gather support. Starting with my boss, which meant bringing up her past theft of the Seeing Stone. Here's hoping I didn't get myself fired in the process.

7

It was with some trepidation that I headed to work on Monday morning, bracing myself for a potentially uncomfortable conversation with my boss. I didn't see another way around it, though—if she knew anything that might help me argue my father's case against the hunters, I had to ask her about her own trial for the theft of the Seeing Stone.

Nathan, Erin and I had discussed all our options throughout the weekend, while Alissa and I had spent yesterday brewing up potions. Okay, that was mostly Alissa. I still wasn't quite accomplished enough at complex potions and spells to want to risk messing something up with the stakes so high. Instead, I'd been practising using glamour. Not just turning invisible, but making myself look like someone else as well. Glamour wouldn't fool the Inquisitor, but if I needed to go into Eric's house myself, I'd have to go in as someone else. Erin didn't mind me pretending to be her, but that plan was a last resort. Ideally, I needed to be as far away as possible from Eric's house when the theft took place so I wouldn't be suspected.

As for my boss? I decided to speak to her daughter first. Bethan might not know of her mother's theft of the Seeing Stone, but I might as well ask a friend before risking my job.

To my dismay, however, I was the last to arrive at work despite the fact that I'd intentionally left home earlier than usual. Bethan was hard at work already, while Rob had made me coffee just the way I liked it. Lizzie waved at me across the desk while the printer chirped a greeting. I smiled back, resigning myself to speaking to the boss and not to her daughter. I'd rather not have an audience, and however unappealing the idea of asking Veronica about an uncomfortable part of her past might be, I needed answers.

"I'll be back in a minute," I told the others, ducking out into the reception area and waving at Callie on the way through. Then I walked to Veronica's office and knocked on the door.

"Come in!" she said.

I opened the door. "It's me. Um, I wanted to talk to you."

Veronica's office looked the same as before, with flowers blooming in each corner and trees stretching from floor to ceiling. Now I looked more closely, the shiny quality to everything was disconcertingly similar to the fairy's cottage in the woods, except created by witch magic and not glamour.

I sat down on the same tree stump as before, while Veronica faced me across the desk. My heartbeat quickened, my mind scrabbling to come up with a tactful way to bring up the subject of the Seeing Stone. I dismissed the notion of asking why she'd taken it outright, since it was none of my business, and it was my dad's trial I needed to know about. Not hers.

"What is it, Blair?" she asked.

"Um, I don't know if you've talked to Madame Grey lately, but she's been helping me look into my dad's imprisonment in the LPFP," I began. "We found the report from his trial, and it sounds like he was arrested for stealing a Seeing Stone from the regional witch coven. Since you knew my mum, I wondered if you knew anything about his trial. I don't really know much about Seeing Stones, but I'd be grateful for anything you can tell me."

She drummed her fingers on the desk. "I don't recall hearing the details of your father's crime, but I imagine the coven would react badly to their Seeing Stone being taken, especially by an outsider. It's one of a kind."

"I heard," I said. "I also heard anyone can use it to see into the future. Is it true?"

"Who told you that?"

"Old Ava," I said. "Though I'm not sure she's the most reliable source of information…"

"Perhaps not, but it's true," she said. "Anyone can use the Seeing Stone if they so desire. It's not a hundred percent accurate, of course, but it's the closest anyone in the magical world has to true future sight."

"More than a crystal ball?" I said. "Is that why my dad might have taken it? Obviously, I haven't spoken to him, but I don't know why he would have wanted to steal it. My mum was dead by that point, and I was living outside of the paranormal world."

Never mind why Veronica had taken it—why had my *dad* wanted to see the future? What had been important enough for him to risk his freedom for? I mean, if he'd wanted to know if he'd escape the hunters, he'd drawn their attention by stealing it in the first place. Something definitely didn't add up, that was for sure.

"I didn't know your father," she said. "Maybe ask the regional witch council at next week's meeting."

She knows about the meeting? "Um, I'm not sure I'm invited."

She looked up at me. "Really? You trained the Head Witch. You ought to be there."

I fidgeted in my seat. "I didn't. I mean, Rita trained her more than I did. Anyway, I'm not sure I belong there, and I doubt mentioning my dad was arrested will endear me to the other council members."

She was still looking at me oddly. "Perhaps not, but you ought to ask Madame Grey. She'll agree you should be there, I don't doubt.."

I looked down. "I can mention it, then. Anyway, she's busy looking into who was involved in arresting my dad. I know the Seeing Stone was valuable, but it doesn't sound like he did anything that warranted a lifelong sentence, right?"

"You'll have to ask the people who were involved in the trial," she said. "If it were up to me, I'd never have enacted such an unjust punishment. I'm sure Madame Grey will be able to help you find out why they made that decision."

"Yeah." I hesitated. "The meeting, though… did you know the Inquisitor is sending someone there to represent him?"

"He is?" She wore a thoughtful expression. "Is he up to his old tricks?"

"Yeah." I swallowed. "He also tried to recruit me."

"And you said no?" Her gaze fixed on me. "I'd hate to lose one of my best employees."

"I haven't seen him since he made the offer, but I'm going to turn him down," I said. "I think he's trying to manipulate me, though, and I wanted to warn you in case he came here. He definitely still has Fairy Falls on his list. Madame Grey thinks so, too. I didn't want everyone to be taken unawares."

"Of course, Blair," she said. "I appreciate you letting me know. And you'll always have a place here."

My eyes stung. "Thank you."

I didn't need to know about her own experience with stealing the Seeing Stone. The important thing was that she believed my dad's sentence was unjust, and she knew the Inquisitor had marked me as a target.

As for the Inquisitor? If Madame Grey did agree that I had a place at the meeting with the regional witch council, maybe I'd be in with a shot at exposing the Inquisitor as a fraud after all.

———

After work, I dodged Rob's attempts to invite me to a werewolf party at the New Moon pub tonight and waited for Bethan to leave the office before waylaying her by the door.

"Hey, Bethan," I said. "Can I talk to you for a moment?"

"Are you going to tell me why you wanted to speak to

the boss earlier?" she asked. "I take it it's about some top-secret fairy business?"

"Not exactly," I said. "The hunters are trying to recruit me, and I may be about to do something that'll really annoy them."

"So you think they'll come here," she surmised. "To Fairy Falls."

"I think that was already their plan." I glanced behind us to make sure our co-workers were out of earshot. "It's okay if you don't want to answer, but… but I wanted to ask you a question about Veronica."

She raised a brow. "Something you couldn't ask her yourself?"

"Lost my nerve," I admitted. "My dad was jailed in the LPFP for stealing something from the regional witch coven. I heard your mother stole the exact same thing, yet she didn't receive the same punishment."

Her eyes rounded. "What? How would you know that?"

"The hunters," I explained. "Nathan's brother told me, and I assume the Inquisitor was the one who told him so that he'd have something to taunt me with. I won't tell anyone else if you don't want me to."

She looked away. "My mother did some absurd things after she split up with my father. Maybe stealing was one of them, but I don't know what she stole."

"She took the Seeing Stone from the regional witch coven," I clarified. "You know, it can be used to see the future."

"Oh." She groaned. "Yeah. I can see her doing that. I'm guessing that's why she spent some time in the hunters' jail at one point."

"Some time, but not a lifetime imprisonment," I said. "Someone saw to it that my dad was punished much more harshly for the same crime."

"Meaning the Inquisitor?" she guessed. "Wait, you said he wanted to recruit you? Even though he arrested your dad?"

"To be honest, I'm confused on that one, too, but I haven't actually spoken to the guy in a long time," I admitted. "I'm just giving everyone a warning that he might come back to Fairy Falls to visit me in person. I'm hoping he doesn't target Eldritch & Co, but I frankly have no idea what he wants from me."

"But—you think your dad was punished unfairly?" she asked. "Because if you want to make a stand against the hunters, I'm not sure even Madame Grey would have the clout to overturn their sentence. Is that why Alissa mentioned she was brewing potions all weekend?"

"No, that's more of a precaution." *And preparation for an attempted robbery.* "Anyway, Veronica thinks I should go to the regional witch council meeting next week and talk to them. I haven't asked Madame Grey yet."

"With the Head Witch, right?" she said. "I don't see why Madame Grey would say no. Just be careful with the hunters, all right? We can't afford to lose another co-worker."

"Your mum said the same," I said. "I'm not that much of an asset to Dritch & Co, surely."

"Hey, the hunters want you for a reason."

Pretty sure it's not to do with my expertise in all things magical. I decided not to voice that thought aloud. As for the regional witch council meeting, I might as well talk to Madame Grey and see what she thought of it.

I didn't have a magic lesson today, but I went to the witches' headquarters anyway. I hadn't checked in with Madame Grey about her search for information on my dad's trial and the fairies since our last conversation, and while now I knew a little more thanks to Veronica, it was Madame Grey who had the authority to ask the regional witch council which of their members had helped the Inquisitor ensure my dad had faced a lifelong jail sentence.

I walked to Madame Grey's office and halted outside the door when I saw it was slightly open. Rita exited a moment later, and Madame Grey peered over her desk and spotted me outside.

"Blair," she said. "Do come in."

I walked into her office and closed the door behind me. "I just wondered if you had an update for me. On my dad's trial and the Seeing Stone, I mean."

"Not yet," she said. "If the hunters realise I'm examining their past cases, then they might accelerate their plan to come here in person. I will not endanger everyone unnecessarily."

"I know," I said. "I just wanted to check. Er, I also heard there's a meeting with the regional witch council next week and Rebecca will be expected to go."

"Yes, that's true," she said. "I intend to ask Rebecca herself whether she wants to attend, but Rita and I are working on a plan."

Her tone implied she had quite enough going on already, so telling her about our plan to get the Pixie-Glass from Nathan's brother did not strike me as a wise idea.

"Okay," I said. "Um, hypothetically, if I wanted to do

something risky, should I tell you first or would that make the situation worse?"

"If you're referring to what you and my granddaughter are plotting, please keep me out of it."

Thought so. Madame Grey had to seem impartial if she wanted to avoid the hunters' attention, and besides, we'd already prepared as well as we possibly could. All that was left to us was luck. Not of the Lucky Latte variety, either, though I'd debated getting one of those before launching our plan to get our hands on the Pixie-Glass. I'd concluded it wasn't worth the potential backlash. The odds of things going spectacularly wrong were too high already.

I left Madame Grey's office and went home. When I reached the house, I found Nina on her way out, sidestepping a group of bright flowers growing around the doorstep.

"What's all this for?" asked Nina. "Why are these weird plants all over the garden?"

We're fairy-proofing the house. Or rather, Inquisitor-proofing. If he could fly like me, he'd easily be able to get inside regardless, but it didn't hurt to have extra defences in place in case he or one of his fellow fairies decided to pay me an unexpected visit. We'd opted against using the potentially lethal bright purple flowers in case the pixie or I ran into them by mistake, but the flowers we'd chosen to plant outside would give a nasty rash to any fairy who decided to approach the house without an invitation.

The problem, of course, was that anything fairy-proof was also Blair-proof, and I was the one who actually lived here. Based on past experience, I'd probably end up falling into the bushes myself at some point.

"Just a project of ours," I said vaguely. "Um, be careful with the flowers."

The pixie was confined to the flat, so I expected to find him zipping all over the ceiling when I entered the living room. Instead, he sat perched on a shelf as Alissa stood over a bubbling cauldron, while Samuel the vampire sat on the sofa, reading a book. The dark-skinned vampire shot me a fanged smile when I walked into the living room.

"Oh," I said. "Hi, Samuel."

He returned to his book. "Pleasure, Blair."

Does he know our plan? I'd been getting better at blocking the vampire from reading my thoughts, but that didn't mean I wanted him to know about our scheme to get the Pixie-Glass from Nathan's brother. If he hadn't already read it from Alissa's mind, anyway.

"How's the potions?" I asked Alissa, whose hair stood up in all directions from the steam. The pixie watched her from a high shelf above her head, though the cats kept their distance, probably remembering the accidental invisibility incident a few months ago.

"Not too bad." She gave the cauldron stir and turned around. "Samuel wanted to see me, and I didn't want to leave my potion unattended, so I invited him here. How was work?"

"Not too bad." I hadn't been fired at least, but I was still at a loss as to how to handle the business with the regional witch council. Better to get the Pixie-Glass first, so my dad would be able to offer his advice.

My phone buzzed with a message from Nathan: *my dad has agreed to meet with you this evening.*

"This evening!" I yelped.

Alissa startled, her elbow knocking into the cauldron. She steadied it with her hand. "What is it?"

"Nathan's dad's coming to town," I said. "Um, are the potions ready?"

"Some of them." She indicated several bottles on the counter. "I was brewing backups, but… do you mean his dad is coming here now? What time?"

"Good question." I texted Nathan back asking as much. "You still up for this?"

"What kind of question is that?" she said. "Is Erin?"

"I assume she is." I caught sight of Samuel watching me with his head tilted on one side. "I take it you told your boyfriend, Alissa? Or he read your thoughts?"

"I respect your privacy," said the vampire, "but yes, she told me you have some foolish notion of stealing from the local hunters' branch."

"Not exactly," I said. "There's something important which happens to be in the hands of Nathan's brother. We need to borrow it for a couple of hours without him realising it's gone."

The upside was that the Inquisitor wasn't here in person. The downside was that he wouldn't be far behind his new assistant, and he'd doubtless be watching for me to make a move against him. That meant my best bet was to keep his eyes on me, while my friends moved behind the scenes and swiped the Pixie-Glass. Nathan had found his brother's new address in the neighbouring town, and Alissa had brewed up a transportation spell, plus a couple of invisibility potions for Erin and the others to use. I could already glamour myself invisible, but I wouldn't be going to Eric's house in person. Instead, I'd be using my glamour to make an accurate substitute with which to replace the real Pixie-Glass while it was gone.

While I'd never used glamour to create a replica of an existing object, I'd been practising all weekend. While I was reasonably confident that Eric wouldn't notice the glass was a fake at first, the Inquisitor was another story, which meant I had to be ready to contact my dad immediately upon getting my hands on the Pixie-Glass.

Samuel rose to his feet. "Am I correct in thinking you intend to meet with this representative of the hunters in order to deflect their attention from your friends while they embark on this daring mission of yours?"

"Pretty much." I checked Nathan's reply. "Oh. Nathan's dad wants to meet at the town's border. Same place I saw him last time."

Not a place of pleasant memories, considering it was at that very spot that I'd found out my mother was dead, and Mr Harker had been the last person to see her alive. No doubt he'd had exactly that in mind when he'd chosen to meet me there, unless he was reluctant to set foot in the town itself. Yet I'd already sworn to myself that I would do this.

Samuel studied me. "You plan to meet with him alone?"

"I have to," I said. "Nathan will be close by. But if you're volunteering to help us out, the more the merrier."

"The hunters are not fans of my people either," he said. "Tell me what you need me to do."

I looked between him and Alissa. "If it turns out we can't get back into Eric's house without drawing attention, you're stealthier than the rest of us put together."

"Miaow," Sky announced.

"I know you're stealthy, too," I said to the little cat. "But I'm not sure you can carry a Pixie-Glass around single-handedly, even a fake one."

"Miaow," he said.

"You're still playing an important role in our plan," I reassured him. "If Eric is still around, we need to lure him away from his house."

"Pixie-Glass," said Samuel. "What is that?"

As Alissa began to explain, my phone buzzed with a message from Erin: *we're doing this tonight?*

I hesitated, my finger hovering over the screen, and then said, *yes.*

Nathan's father had agreed to talk to me. Now all we had to do was put our plan into motion.

8

I headed to the town's border, waiting for an update from my friends. I flew through the woods alongside the lake, and then put my wings away as soon as I was out in the open in full view of the border. Mr Harker would have the exact same level of disdain for me whether I met him as a fairy or a witch, but it made me feel more secure to be meeting him as a human. Even if it did make it harder to make a quick getaway to fetch my friends to back me up if it turned out he'd brought half the hunters with him.

Erin texted me: *He's out. Going in.*

Good luck, I texted back.

Eric's house didn't have any magical defences on it, according to Erin, but the Pixie-Glass might. I wouldn't put anything past the Inquisitor, after all. Alissa had loaned most of the potions she'd brewed to Erin and Nathan, since they had no magical abilities of their own. Sky was with them as well, but of course he couldn't text me and tell me how they were getting on. Samuel, meanwhile, had agreed to act as our backup in case Erin and Nathan ran into difficulty in her brother's house.

My nerves jangled as I approached the far side of the woods. I'd asked Nathan to warn the werewolves there'd be activity in the area, just in case, but I'd still prefer not to run into Chief Donovan.

Nathan's father stood alone at the border, waiting for me. With dark hair and a broad frame, he resembled his children strikingly; most of them had taken after him, it seemed, but the scowl on his face more closely resembled Eric than Nathan. I halted in front of him, trying not to let my apprehension show. I'd found Mr Harker hanging around here before, watching the town, but he'd never given me a real explanation for his interest in keeping an eye on Fairy Falls from afar. *I hope he's not spying on us for the Inquisitor, too.*

"You wanted to speak to me, Blair," he said.

"I did." I drew in a breath. "This is going to sound weird, but well... I got a note from the Inquisitor inviting me to join the hunters."

His brows shot up. "Really?"

I held out the note so he could read it, figuring that he wouldn't take my word as adequate enough proof. "Yeah. It's the second time he's asked me to join. He did the same a few months ago and I said no because I already have a job, but I wanted to see him this time so we can talk in person. The thing is, I have no idea whereabouts he's based, so I thought I'd come to you instead."

"This is indeed his handwriting," he observed. "I cannot fathom *why* he'd want to recruit you to work for us. We are a disciplined force of order. You are an agent of chaos."

That's nice. "He seemed interested in my skills as a fairy."

His jaw twitched at the word. Did he know about the Inquisitor's true nature? Nathan had said he didn't, but perhaps it was possible for me to shake his faith in his former boss.

"I doubt it," he said. "Perhaps he wished to remove you from Fairy Falls due to the trouble you've unleashed."

I didn't rise to his bait. "I can tell when people are lying, and he wasn't. He definitely wanted to hire me."

Never mind that with the Inquisitor, my lie-sensing power didn't work and nor did my ability to tell what type of paranormal he was. Nathan's dad wouldn't know any better, after all.

"So you can." He looked me over. "Is there a point to this, or did you simply want to ask me to arrange a meeting with him? Why not call him instead?"

"Because it struck me as suspicious that he wanted to hire me at all," I said. "Okay, I guess that the ability to use glamour to make myself look like any other person—even pretend to be human—must be in high demand for the hunters. Buck is a fairy, too, so I wouldn't be the only one the hunters recruited."

"Buck is no longer working for us," he growled. "He and Erin both turned their backs on our cause, largely because of *your* influence. Do you expect me to believe you're skilled enough to be sought out by the Inquisitor himself? I certainly wouldn't hire you."

"I'm not asking you to hire me," I said. "The Inquisitor didn't actually tell me why he's taken an interest in me. I assumed since you have direct contact with him, you might have an idea, but I guess I was wrong."

His glower deepened. "The Inquisitor is wiser than most of us. I'd thank you to show him a little more respect."

"Eric paid Nathan a visit over the weekend, too," I added. "He said the Inquisitor promoted him to some kind of special ambassador to represent him at the regional witch council meeting. That surprised me. I'm not sure I'd have chosen *him* for an important job, let's put it that way."

His jaw tensed. "Eric needs to learn to keep his mouth shut when it comes to important matters."

"I thought the hunters were masters of discipline." Caution warred with the need to know the truth. "I wonder what made the Inquisitor pick him and not you or Jay?"

If I pushed too far, then I'd regret it, but how many hints did I need to drop for him to realise his boss wasn't all he seemed? If I was any more blatant, I'd be waving a banner with the words *The Inquisitor is a Fairy* on it in neon glittering writing. At least I'd effectively distracted him so that he wouldn't have the faintest clue that my friends were stealing from Eric right now.

The real question was, how much *did* he know about the Inquisitor's secrets?

Mr Harker shook his head. "You called me here to waste my time, Blair. If you don't mind, I have more important matters to attend to."

"I'm sure you do," I said. "I only wanted to know how much input the Inquisitor has in the recruitment process, and if I'm the only fairy he's approached."

"Then I'm sure he'll be interested to discuss the matter

with you in person, Blair." He gave me a disdainful look. "Good day."

He walked away without another word. *That went well.* At least I'd momentarily had my mind taken off my friends' risky venture, but now my worries came surging back. I waited until I was certain he wasn't going to turn around before retracing my steps down the path leading alongside the forest.

My phone buzzed. A message from Erin—*There's a problem. We need you. Meet me by the lake.*

Oh, no. What had gone wrong? I sent a reply asking her what she meant, then I ducked into the trees and brought out my wings with a snap of my fingers. I flew as fast as I could, towards our chosen meeting point along-side the lake, and spotted Erin approaching along with Sky. When she saw me, she held up a long piece of glass the size of a small mirror.

The Pixie-Glass. The mission had been a success, it seemed. "What's the problem?"

"Nathan ran into some trouble." She turned the glass over, revealing its glittering surface. "We got it, though. Your friend has the replacement, right?"

"What do you mean by trouble?" I looked down when Sky meowed and butted my ankle. *What did Nathan do?*

"He ran into a trap and told me to take the glass and run," she said. "He pretty much ordered me to leave him behind."

Oh, no. "I'll find Alissa. Is she at the clearing?"

"Last I checked." She and I walked through the forest to the clearing where we'd chosen to set up the trans-portation spell. Alissa, who stood guard over the circle of herbs, nodded to both of us.

"You're back early, Blair," she said. "No problems?"

"No, but what kind of trap did Nathan run into?" I asked.

"Relax, Blair. I'm sure he's fine." She held out the mirror we'd bought for me to glamour into a replacement for the Pixie-Glass. "Use your glamour on this so we can put it in place of the real thing."

Worry squirmed inside me, but it wouldn't do any good for me to run to Eric's house without the fake Pixie-Glass to use as a substitute. Trying my best to keep my fear in check, I fixed my gaze on the mirror, calling on my fairy magic. Then I snapped my fingers, and glitter flowed from my fingers to the mirror. Shimmering, the mirror elongated, turning into an exact replica of the Pixie-Glass. I took it from Alissa and tucked it under my arm. "Good enough. I'm going in. Can you keep the Pixie-Glass hidden until I get back?"

"Of course." Alissa rolled her eyes. "The whole point in all this was to avoid you having to go to Eric's house in person, Blair."

"I know, but I'm not leaving him there." Eric might be his brother, but if the Inquisitor showed up and figured out our plan, I wouldn't leave Nathan to face him alone.

The circle of herbs forming the transportation spell remained intact, and I stepped into the centre, waving my wand as I did so. Sky jumped in behind me, and we vanished.

We landed in a living room, presumably Eric's. I spotted Nathan right away behind a sheet of what looked like a transparent glass, frozen to the spot as though trapped in an invisible web.

"Nathan?" I walked up to him. "Did the Inquisitor give your brother some kind of security spell?"

Sky meowed, padding up to Nathan's frozen form. Nathan's mouth moved, but I couldn't hear a word he said. I held up my wand, hesitating to take aim. I didn't want to hit Nathan by accident, but the weird barrier didn't seem to have a beginning or end.

"Hang in there," I told Nathan. "I'll get you out."

I trod around the shimmering barrier which resembled a kind of forcefield. *It's fairy magic.*

*And t*hanks to my fairy and witch magic, I could see through any fairy glamour.

I squinted at the invisible barrier and spotted a shimmering patch at the very end. *There it is.*

The Inquisitor would have to try harder next time. With a snap of my fingers, the spell began to unravel, layer by layer.

When the barrier fell down, Nathan stepped forwards and embraced me. "Wow, Blair. That was…"

"Fairy magic," I said. "The Inquisitor's, I reckon."

"No doubt," he said. "We'd better go."

"Hang on." I held up the copy of the Pixie-Glass. "Where do I put this?"

"Here." He indicated the spot where he'd been standing. "Just lean it against the wall there. You did a great job —it looks just like the real thing."

"I hope it lasts," I said. "Okay. Stand close to me."

Sky hopped onto my shoulder. I waved my wand, and we vanished and reappeared in the forest clearing.

It looked just the same as we'd left it, except Alissa now stood across from us, with Samuel at her side.

"I thought you needed my help," the vampire said.

"The barrier was made of fairy magic, so I took care of it," I said. "Thanks for offering anyway. And Alissa—thanks for everything."

"Anytime." She started to dismantle the piles of herbs forming the transportation spell as I stepped out of the circle. "Erin went to meet Buck by the lake."

With the Pixie-Glass. My heart leapt in my chest at the notion that I'd have the chance speak to my dad. For real. I'd waited for far too long. I all but ran to the meeting spot by the lake, where Erin and Buck stood waiting for me.

"Do you have any idea how many merpeople have poked their heads out of the lake to stare at us?" she said. "Even the elves have been wandering around."

"As long as they didn't see the Pixie-Glass, it's fine," I said. "The fake glass is back at Eric's house, so now we need to use the real thing. Where is it?"

She reached into the bushes and pulled out the glass. "All right, then, work your magic."

"Uh…" I took the glass from her with careful movements. Now I looked closer, it didn't seem to have an obvious way to turn it on, and its surface remained opaque. "Does anyone know how to use this thing?"

"Maybe use your fairy magic?" Erin snapped her fingers in demonstration.

"All right, I'll do that." Gingerly, I carried the glass through to the clearing, where Alissa had finished moving the herbs out of the way. "I think my dad might freak out if he sees all of you standing in the background, though."

"Give her some space," Nathan said, and I felt a rush of gratitude towards him.

I placed the glass down in the clearing and sat down in front of it. My nerves spiked, my heartbeat racing in my ears. It was now or never. Before I could lose my nerve, I faced the glass and snapped my fingers. Its surface shimmered, and then I found myself looking through a window into the inside of a room with plain walls. There, someone sat on a metal chair, facing me, as though expecting my appearance.

It wasn't my father.

Blythe's mother gave a nod of satisfaction. "Hello, Blair. I wondered when we'd finally have the chance to talk to one another again."

9

I gaped at Mrs Dailey, whose severe face appeared as clear in the glass as though she sat in the same room as me. I found myself fervently glad I hadn't been at home and had chosen to use the Pixie-Glass here in the clearing instead.

I'd known she was the person who held the Pixie-Glass I'd originally been searching for at the market, but not that she'd be waiting for me on the other side when I tried to contact my dad. Especially as she was supposed to be under high security. Was nobody keeping an eye on her at all?

"Aren't you going to speak?" she asked. "I thought you were keen to communicate with the LPFP. You certainly went through a lot of trouble to get in touch, given the rarity of fairy artefacts such as the one you're using. In fact, most are in the hands of the hunters, I believe."

She knew. She must know I'd stolen the Pixie-Glass, and now she could ruin everything for me. If she told the

Inquisitor—and she definitely had direct access to him—it didn't matter how well I'd covered my tracks. Everything would be ruined.

Or that's what she wanted me to think, anyway. Regardless of how close she might seem, Mrs Dailey couldn't harm me, and I wouldn't discount the opportunity she'd brought me to ask all the questions I wanted to about my family.

"I was hoping to speak to someone I actually like," I said. "I'm surprised it isn't Blythe you wanted to talk to. Or Rebecca. Not me."

Her eyes narrowed with annoyance. "I wouldn't push me, Blair. I can still make your life difficult even from my current position."

"My life is already a nightmare." I surprised myself by laughing. "You haven't the slightest idea how much you've missed, but believe me, I'd pretty much forgotten about you."

Not exactly the truth, though she hadn't been my biggest worry for a long time. Compared to the Inquisitor, she scared me less and less by the day.

She leaned closer to the glass. "Then you haven't been asking the right questions. In case you've forgotten, the two of us are related, Blair, via your traitor of a mother."

"Not something I like to think about, believe me." I managed to reel in my words before they got me into any more trouble. "I've already spoken to my mother's ghost. It's my dad I want to know more about. Specifically, who from the regional witch council conspired with the Inquisitor to see to it that he never walked free again."

"Oh, that information is easily available," she said. "I

don't doubt Madame Grey already has it. But knowing who was responsible won't help you do anything about his punishment."

So she'd guessed I wanted to free my dad. Not that it made a difference if she knew, considering she'd already thrown a wrench in my plans to contact him. Yet she wasn't all-knowing, no matter what she said. Everything she knew was entirely dependent on what the Inquisitor chose to share with her from the other side of her cell door.

"You don't have a clue what Madame Grey knows," I told her. "Why'd they even give you the Pixie-Glass?"

"Being a personal friend of the Inquisitor's has its advantages," she said. "I believe your father once possessed a similar item himself, though he had it taken away from him when he stopped behaving himself. Now he's under the tightest security possible."

Then he didn't have the Pixie-Glass any longer, as I'd suspected from the instant she'd appeared in his place. Yet it still hurt to see my last hopes go up in smoke. How could I figure out how to free my dad without input from the man himself? He alone knew all the details of his trial. All I had now was access to a woman I'd hoped never to see again.

"Forget him," said Mrs Dailey. "Your father never would have put you first, Blair. He avoided making contact with you even when he walked free, too ashamed of the chaos he and your mother had left behind them. Why do you think he never told you the identity of his real family, nor his royal status?"

Anger exploded within me. "I already know he used to

be a prince before he was exiled from the fairies." The Inquisitor had probably told her the details, but that didn't lessen my growing fury at both of them.

"If you already know, then why do you need to ask him?" she said. "Forget him, Blair. You don't have to get involved in the fairies' games."

Rage made me speechless for a moment. Then I forced out the words. "You know what I don't understand? The Inquisitor is a fairy, yet you hate the fairies. What's so bad about my mother falling in love with one of them if you've allied with the fairies yourself?"

"Not all fairies are the same," she said. "Your father and his kin are exiles and traitors, like the beasts who sought refuge in that town you call home."

My shoulders stiffened. *The fairies who founded Fairy Falls. Was that what she meant? Surely not.* She hadn't been alive back then. She might have access to more information than most people, but she wasn't immortal. Or all-knowing.

But the Inquisitor... does he know?

"That's rich coming from you," I said. "Calling someone a beast, I mean. Besides, whoever my mum fell in love with is none of your business."

"I beg to differ," she said. "Your mother was well aware of our family history when she met your father. If anything, she enjoyed stamping on our legacy."

My heart climbed into my throat. "What legacy?"

"What else?" she said. "You and I are descendants of the original coven who founded Fairy Falls. That is our legacy."

"But," I said numbly, "that means..."

"Yes, Blair," she said softly.

That meant my ancestors had driven the fairies out of Fairy Falls. Blythe's, too. They were the reason Conor Underwood was in hiding, the reason my dad had been unable to find anywhere safe to take me as a baby… and the reason for my own outcast status.

No wonder Mrs Dailey had hated my mother for pursuing my father, considering how far back her coven's hatred of the fairies must have gone. And no wonder the other fairies had nursed such a hatred towards my dad for choosing to be with Tanith Wildflower. I could almost understand why Dill had chosen the hunters over the witches, as he'd known Fairy Falls had once belonged to the fairies before the witches had seen to it that they left. Yet I'd never have imagined it might be *my* ancestors who were responsible for driving them out.

It hadn't been Madame Grey or the modern covens who'd been responsible, but they wouldn't be able to do anything to right the wrongs our ancestors had committed, not with the most powerful of all the fairies working against us. From the smile on Mrs Dailey's face, she knew I'd figured out the impossibility of resolving the issue.

"You mean to say the Inquisitor is completely fine with working with you, knowing your ancestors drove his out of town?" I asked.

"Why wouldn't he be?" she said. "He is a fairy noble, not an exiled beast, and the exiles gave him and the hunters nothing but trouble. Our ancestors banished them from the town of Fairy Falls, and for that, he is grateful."

I clenched my hands. "Then why does he want me to work for the hunters? No matter what my witch ancestors did to help him, the other half of my ancestors are the very fairies he hates so much."

"Therein lies your dilemma, Blair," she said. "You must choose one or the other. Personally, I'd pick the winning side, but I'm not you."

My hands clenched. "You know, you're doing a pretty good job of pretending to be on the winning team for someone facing a life sentence behind bars."

She gave a soft laugh. "Blair, you must know this cage is for appearances only. I still enjoy most of the privileges I did when I was free, with the bonus of being safely away from the covens."

Her words rang with truth, secure in the knowledge that I wouldn't be able to expose her to the authorities. The man in charge of her sentence was her ally, and he'd offered her this chance to taunt me so there'd be no doubt who was really calling the shots.

I couldn't stand to look at her for another moment, so I snapped my fingers. Her face disappeared from the glass, yet my dad didn't appear in her place. Not even when I spoke his name, over and over. *Braden Eventide.* No matter how hard I tried, I was unable to reach him.

My eyes burned with tears and I sank into a sitting position once again. In the blurred glass, I saw Nathan's reflection approach me, a moment before he crouched down and put an arm around my shoulder. "Are you okay, Blair?"

I shook my head. "I don't know. There's just so much..." How could I even begin to tell him what my ancestors had done? His own family had less than scrupulous ties, but being related to the people who'd driven the fairies out of town? I couldn't wrap my head around what it meant for me, and for the fairies in general.

"I heard some of it," he said, an apologetic note in his voice. "The Inquisitor clearly wants to play both sides of your family against one another."

"He's also granting Mrs Dailey privileges she shouldn't have," I said. "She pretty much said she's free to do whatever she likes. That wasn't part of her sentence."

"We can certainly challenge that, but with the Inquisitor himself in charge of her case, it'll be difficult," he said. "I suspect he's been duping everyone for years, and not just with his glamoured human disguise, either."

"I told your dad," I said. "I mean, I dropped a million hints that the Inquisitor is a fraud who's lying to everyone. Not sure if he picked up on it or not."

"I suspect that even if you did get through to him, my father has been involved with the hunters for too long to easily be convinced to turn on them," he said, a note of sadness to his voice. "It's his whole life. My brothers', too. Erin and I both know from personal experience how hard it is to walk away."

I looked around and saw Erin and Buck had vanished from sight. Alissa and Samuel, too. Only Sky remained, padding over to my side. "Miaow."

I stroked his head. "Miaow yourself. I don't suppose you have any advice for me?"

"Miaow."

"I'm going to take that to mean, 'screw the Inquisitor, forget Mrs Dailey, and keep trying to get your dad off the hook'," I said. "I can't reach him with the Pixie-Glass, though. Mrs Dailey told me the Inquisitor has seen to it that he has zero contact with the outside world."

"I'm sorry, Blair," Nathan said. "I suspected the Inquisitor might find a way to intervene, but not that he'd allow Mrs Dailey to speak to you directly."

"I bet she asked to have one last chance to taunt me," I said. "I also have no idea what I'm actually going to say to the Inquisitor when he comes to speak to me."

"You're expecting him soon?" asked Nathan.

"I may have taunted your dad a bit when I mentioned his offer of employment."

"He probably deserved it." Nathan drew me into an embrace, and I gladly let him hold me. "You did a brave thing there. We should head home."

"Yeah." I drew back from him and stood, brushing fragments of leaves from my knees, while Nathan picked up the Pixie-Glass. "We need to put this thing back before your brother notices it's missing."

"I'll handle it," he said. "Now you've removed that defensive spell, it shouldn't be too hard."

I hoped the glamour I'd used on the fake Pixie-Glass had held up, but I didn't have the energy to argue with Nathan about risking his safety again. My mind was stuck on Mrs Dailey's taunts. Had Blythe known our ancestors had driven the fairies out of town? Unlikely, but the notion of convincing her to help me right the wrongs of our ancestors was laughable. Unlike me, she didn't have a direct link to the fairies herself and had nothing to gain from helping me. She just wanted to keep Rebecca safe, and I knew better than to add to the young Head Witch's worries by telling her about our family history.

Mrs Dailey had already uprooted *my* world. I didn't need to give her the chance to get at her daughters again, too.

Nathan and I met up with Erin and Buck on the walk home. I didn't know how much they'd overheard of my conversation with Mrs Dailey, but they knew I hadn't been able to talk to my dad. The Inquisitor had seen to that.

"He knew," I murmured. "He knew I was going to contact my dad today. He told Mrs Dailey. That's why she was expecting me."

Nathan didn't answer, but he must know I was right, as much as I wished I wasn't. The Inquisitor had known I'd called a meeting with Nathan's father, and it wouldn't have taken much more guesswork for him to figure out I'd planned to use it as a cover for my theft of the Pixie-Glass. He was too clever, too many steps ahead of us. And now my goal seemed further away than ever.

"I'll drop off the Pixie-Glass at Eric's place,' Nathan offered. "Then we'll head for the Troll's Tavern later this evening."

"Sounds good," said Erin. "We'll make it a double date."

After we parted ways, I took Sky home and checked in with Alissa, who was as shocked and appalled as I'd predicted at the news that Mrs Dailey and the Inquisitor had been ten steps ahead of us. I waited on tenterhooks, checking my phone every few minutes, but Nathan's update on the successful return of the Pixie-Glass came swiftly. It seemed Eric had yet to return home and had no idea two of his siblings had sneaked in and out of his house twice in a single evening, yet my relief was dampened by the loss of my only chance to contact my dad.

As planned, Nathan and I met up with Erin and Buck at the Troll's Tavern. The food revived me a little, as did Erin's loud jokes and general lighthearted attitude, and the laughter came with a reminder of easier times. Before the Inquisitor had infiltrated my life. I wouldn't let him have the last word. I'd already told Nathan's father the truth. Whether he took it to heart was another matter entirely, but it was a start.

Erin prodded me in the arm across the table. "No spacing out, Blair. We'll talk about you-know-who later."

"I don't mind talking about it now," I said. "I had an idea, and I think you'll like it."

She cocked a brow. "Oh?"

"When I spoke with your father, I told him the Inquisitor was lying," I said. "I listed the facts about his boss that don't add up no matter how hard you look at it. I'm hoping he ought to have a long hard think, even if he ends up concluding there's nothing he can do."

"Good on you," said Erin, "but I don't know if that'll take away much of the Inquisitor's influence."

"You know other hunters in the area, though, right?" I asked. "Not just in Fairy Falls, but around the whole region."

"You mean aside from the ones I'm related to?" she said. "Sure. I'm even engaged to one of them."

"I mean, active hunters," I said. "Preferably ones who've met the Inquisitor at least once."

Curiosity gleamed in her eyes. "I'm liking the sound of this. Go on."

"The Inquisitor has been openly lying to everyone," I said. "Not just about who he is, but I bet he's doing worse than giving privileges to certain high-security prisoners he happens to like. I have a feeling more than a few of the hunters would find themselves questioning their future employment if they find out how deeply he's been deceiving them."

"They won't take your word for it, though," said Buck.

"But they'd take ours," said Erin, nudging him. "I can think of at least a few people who'd listen if both of us told them their boss was a crook. Everyone knows he plays favourites."

Comprehension dawned on Nathan, too. "Same here."

"You want us to badmouth the Inquisitor to the other hunters?" asked Buck.

"Way ahead of you," said Erin. "I've already done it a dozen times this week alone."

"I thought so." I nodded to Nathan. "You don't have to go too far with it. Just mention how the Inquisitor has a habit of dancing around the truth. The more people who are primed to see him as a liar, the better."

"I don't disagree, Blair," said Nathan, "but he might retaliate against you if he finds out."

"I know, but he can't deny the truth if we back it up with enough proof," I said. "As long as he has people who are willing to look the other way, he'll stay in power. I bet most hunters will never guess he's a fairy, not in a million years. If the truth comes out, he'll be publicly humiliated. He might even step down."

Despite my lingering exhaustion and fear after my conversations with Mr Harker and Mrs Dailey, a renewed sense of resolve strengthened me at the thought of exposing the Inquisitor as the fraud he truly was. Even with the odds stacked against us.

"Where do we start?" asked Erin. "I guess saying he's a fairy outright will get us laughed at…"

Buck cleared his throat. "Then I'll tell them *I'm* a fairy."

Erin blinked. "You will?"

"They don't know?" I asked. "The other hunters, I mean?"

"Not everyone does," said Buck. "If I spread the word about how I was recruited and then how I found out I wasn't the only fairy they'd targeted, it'll be easy to prove. I mean, if I take my glamour off in front of them, they won't exactly be able to call me a liar."

"You've been practising?" I asked.

He nodded. "Yeah. I thought it might come in handy. Anyway, if everyone already knows the hunters are recruiting fairies while pretending they're all but extinct, it won't seem as far-fetched when it comes out that a fairy is actually in charge of them."

"As for me," said Nathan, "I'll talk to Eric and Jay. I think Eric will be harder to get through to, because he has the Inquisitor's explicit trust."

"Yeah, I figured," I said.

"He's also not very bright," added Erin. "Then again, a lot of the hunters aren't, either. I'll do the rounds of everyone I personally know. Drop hints here and there that the Inquisitor is a massive impostor."

And then? We'd have everyone primed for the revelation, whenever it came. Preferably sooner rather than later.

"What about you, Blair?" asked Buck. "You don't know any hunters."

"No... well, I can always speak to my boss again," I said. "And Madame Grey. Also, Steve, maybe. He and the gargoyles probably have connections among the hunters."

"I can deal with Steve," Nathan said. "What should I tell him?"

"For a start, we need to get the LPFP to take Mrs Dailey's Pixie-Glass away from her," I said. "We also need to get the word out that the Inquisitor is sending representatives to the regional witch council meeting. I need to talk to Madame Grey again, too."

In the meantime? It was about time I had a chat with Blythe.

10

The following morning, the pixie woke me up by dropping glitter onto my head. Thankfully, he hit me and not Nathan. Or Sky, though the cat wasn't in the room. He usually did his own thing when I stayed at Nathan's house rather than hanging out with Nathan's own three cats.

Careful not to wake Nathan, I checked my phone and found a message from Bethan—*work's cancelled today. Mum said we need a break.*

Sending a silent thanks to Veronica, I whispered to the pixie, "What is it?"

The pixie fluttered up to the ceiling, shedding more glitter. I got out of bed and shoved my feet into slippers before heading downstairs. The pixie led me outside, where the silent figure of Vincent the vampire stood watching Nathan's house.

I started at the leader of the town's vampires. "Um. Hi."

Of all the people I'd expected to see after yesterday's escapades, Vincent wasn't one of them. Mostly because I'd assumed he'd decided to sit this one out. The vampires had an annoying habit of avoiding any conflict which didn't directly affect them, and their leader most of all.

"Hello, Blair," he said.

"Is there any reason you were staring up at Nathan's house while I was asleep?" I asked.

"I asked your friend here to wake you," he said, indicating the pixie. "I was also having a fascinating chat with your familiar."

Sky meowed from behind his legs. Oh, right. He and the vampire had been friends before I'd even moved here to Fairy Falls… and come to think of it, there was no way Vincent hadn't known he was a fairy cat.

"Did you know?" The accusing words came out before my brain had quite caught up with me.

"Know what?"

"You know," I said, exasperated. "My ancestors. The witches who drove the fairies out of town. You must have been alive back then."

"Yes, I was, but you can't expect me to know the ancestors of every witch I come across," he said.

"Vincent, I'm the only new witch who's moved here in years," I pointed out. "My mother was notorious, and you knew Blythe and my family were related."

"What did you expect me to do?" he said. "The fairies have been gone for hundreds of years."

"The ones who are left don't like my family, and for good reason, to be honest," I admitted. "Except for my dad, but he's in jail because some other fairies decided to put him there."

"The fairies are not unlike witches in that they are not a united entity," said Vincent. "Those who lived in Fairy

Falls were not the same as the ones who conspired with the witches in order to drive them out."

I shot him a sideways look. "You *did* know. My family—"

"They aren't your family, Blair," he said, an impatient undertone to his voice. "Perhaps I speak out of turn, but we vampires choose the company we keep in the same way that you witches choose your covens. I was under the impression that you chose to join the Meadowsweet Coven, which bears no connection with the coven which founded this town."

"It's still my family history!" I threw up my hands. "At the very least, it would have been nice if I'd learned it from someone other than Mrs Dailey. Besides, it would have helped to know *why* everyone hated my parents so much."

"If one thing has not changed with the years," said the elder vampire, "it is humans' propensity for engendering division based on the pettiest of reasons. Your father did not betray the fairies, nor did your mother betray the witches. They were two of the most honourable people I've heard of, and I regret that I never met them."

My eyes stung, surprise brewing inside me at the vampire's honest words. Honest, because my lie-sensing power didn't react in the slightest. I sought to find the words to reply. "I—Vincent, it doesn't matter how honourable my parents were. The fairies have gone, except the Inquisitor, and there's nothing I can do to change that."

"I beg to differ," he said. "There's a great deal you can do, Blair."

"Like what?" I said. "What am I supposed to do, tell

every rogue fairy in the goblin market they're welcome to move here to Fairy Falls? Dill tried to have me killed because he blamed me for his exile. He blamed my dad, too, so even if by some miracle I get him out of jail, the fairies won't exactly flock to my side."

Not as long as the Inquisitor remained in charge of the hunters in the region, anyway. Though it was still a mystery to me as to why he'd turned on his fellow fairies. I still had a lot to learn about the fairies and their rivalries, though.

Nathan appeared in the doorway behind me. "Oh. Vincent. What is it?"

"Blair and I were just chatting," said the elder vampire. "I'll be seeing you later."

He turned away from the house and vanished from sight with the swift steps of one of the living dead.

"What was that about?" asked Nathan.

I shook my head. "I honestly have no idea at all. Are you working today?"

"Yes, why?"

"I just got a message saying my boss has closed the office today," I explained. "Haven't a clue why, but I can't complain at the timing."

"Maybe she's meeting with Madame Grey and the other witches," said Nathan. "I imagine they have a lot to discuss."

"Yeah, now I've invited the Inquisitor to town." I grimaced. "I need to speak to Blythe, too. And Rebecca… I don't know how to tell her. About our ancestors, I mean."

Rebecca would be heading to school in a bit, but I didn't know whereabouts Blythe was currently living. Maybe her old house held too many memories, but I'd seen her in town more than once, so she must be staying somewhere nearby.

"Does Vincent know the Inquisitor is coming?" he said. "Is that what he wanted to talk about?"

"I think he was having a chat with my cat, actually." I gave Sky a stroke behind the ears. "He's a strange one, isn't he?"

"Miaow," said Sky, which probably meant *speak for yourself.*

I'd need to leave now if I wanted to talk to Rebecca before school, unless I waited until afterwards. But I'd rather speak to Blythe first. She would not be pleased with me if I told her sister about our ancestors without asking her permission. Besides, from what I could guess, Blythe herself hadn't known, which meant the news about our ancestors would be as big a surprise to her as it had been to me.

I started by heading to the witches' headquarters while Nathan went to the police station. There, I made straight for Madame Grey's office and knocked.

"Come in," she said.

I entered. "Sorry to disturb you so early."

"Were you successful?" asked Madame Grey, confirming that she'd suspected the nature of our mission yesterday even if she hadn't been willing to get involved herself.

I suspected even she didn't know about my ancestors' history with the fairies, either, but now I'd have to break the news to everyone who'd welcomed me to Fairy Falls with open arms. Somehow it seemed worse even than admitting I was related to Blythe and her ghastly mother.

"Yeah," I mumbled. "But it didn't turn out the way I hoped."

She lifted her head. "Tell me."

I did so, detailing every part of my conversation with Mrs Dailey and her revelations about our ancestors. Madame Grey was silent for a long moment after I'd finished.

"Your parents were not like their respective families," she said. "As you may have gathered."

"Yeah, my dad's family thought he was a traitor for getting involved with my mother, while her own family probably thought the same of her." I shook my head. "I have no idea where that leaves me, considering my chances of getting my dad out of jail are pretty much zero now. Even if I did, the hunters would probably go after him again. Nobody would help us."

"Not necessarily," she said in sympathetic tones. "Don't forget your father lived on the run for a long while. He had help from others during that time."

"From the elves." And Conor Underwood, too. I needed to speak to him again, for that matter, but I didn't know how to tell him about my mother's ancestors. He hadn't ever met her, so maybe he didn't realise which coven she was descended from. For all I knew, he'd turn on me if I told him the truth, and then I'd have no fairies willing to support me at all. I was already a stranger to him, and even my father's status as a fairy prince might not cancel out what my mother's family had done.

"Not just the elves," said Madame Grey. "Even your mother's family... I know it might be hard for you to accept, but most of them did not share your ancestors' views on fairies and their kind. Your mother didn't, and nor did *her* mother."

"Mrs Dailey did," I said. "A lot of things make sense about her now. Like her attitude to the covens and why she feels like the other witches owe her their support. What I don't get is why the Inquisitor wanted to work with her anyway. I know she claims not all fairies are alike, but still. He might pretend to be human, but he's still one of them."

"On that matter, she's correct," said Madame Grey. "Not all fairies are alike. That is likely why the Inquisitor agreed to work with her, due to his disdain for his kin. I confess I don't know the intricate details of the fairies' rivalries, but I do know the Inquisitor must not be well-liked among his fellow fairies to have willingly abandoned them and worked against them."

"Yeah, that makes sense," I said. "He hates the other fairies, I mean, so it makes sense that he'd push anti-fairy views onto everyone as long as he can keep his own secret. But I don't know where we can go from here. It doesn't matter if we advertise the town as being open to fairies, because the other fairies will never want to take the risk as long as he's in the area. Of course, it doesn't help that they hated my dad for choosing to be with my mum, considering they know what her coven did…"

"Not all of them," she said. "The real issue is the hunters—or more specifically, the Inquisitor. He's likely connected to the fairies' departure from town. He's also been head of the region's hunters for long enough that most of them don't remember anything different."

"How long?" I frowned. "He's not that old."

"At least twenty years," she said. "And he worked for

the local branch before then. I would guess that he and Mrs Dailey found a common goal and put aside their history of animosity in order to work together."

"She shouldn't be allowed to keep that Pixie-Glass," I said. "I bet she has contact with other people on the outside, too. Maybe she's even planning on coming back here and trying to bring down the covens again."

"She's welcome to try," said Madame Grey. "In the meantime, I will prepare the best I can. I suggest you do, too."

I fidgeted. "I'm sorry if I made things worse for all of you."

"There's no need to apologise, Blair," she said. "If anything, it helps to have it confirmed that Mrs Dailey has too much freedom. I had an inkling being jailed wouldn't stop her from scheming."

I just wish there was something we could do about it. I mean, the Inquisitor was her biggest supporter, but I wasn't supposed to know they remained allies, and telling the other hunters would only get me into trouble for taking the Pixie-Glass in the first place.

After leaving the witches' headquarters, I wandered aimlessly down the high street until I found myself passing the bright windows of the Enchantment Emporium. Next door stood the fortune-teller's shop, which belonged to Violet Layne, the newest seer in town. I hadn't paid her a visit in a while, but she might be able to give me some insight about the Seeing Stone. I couldn't remember the last time I'd felt so lost, and while she'd confirmed I was no seer myself during my last visit, perhaps she'd be able to give me a glimpse into the future, however clouded.

The sign on the door still said, 'Violet Layne: Seer Extraordinaire', but when I entered, found the shop in a less sparse condition than the last time I'd been here. Last time it'd been covered in dust and contained nothing but a crystal ball sitting on a table. Now, plush chairs lined each side of the wooden floor and mirrors shimmered on the walls. I spotted the woman herself at the back, talking to Annabel of all people.

Ava's granddaughter startled at the sight of me. "Oh. Hi, Blair."

"Hey." I looked to Violet Layne. "Don't let me interrupt you."

"I was just leaving," said Annabel. She headed for the door, while I blinked after her in confusion when she walked out into the street.

"Hello, Blair," said Violet. "I expected to see you sooner than this, but it's a nice surprise."

The seer was in her mid-forties, with medium brown skin and curly hair. She wore a long black robe and sparkling earrings, which reflected the crystal ball on her desk.

"Were you doing a reading for Annabel?" I asked.

"We've both been seeing some unusual things in the glass lately," she said. "Strange omens, and downright odd portents."

"I didn't know she was using her Seeing ability." As far as I knew, Annabel hardly acknowledged her talent existed.

"She has no desire to use her skill to make a living as I do," she said, "but it certainly seems to be more active than usual. Maybe the same is true for her grandmother, too. Strange omens plague me. Dark skies… wings…"

A chill raced down my back. Were they seeing visions of what was coming to the town? If it involved the fairies, maybe they were.

"Anyway," she said, "I recall offering you a discount on a reading, Blair. Have you come to take me up on my offer?"

"Well… I could use some advice."

"Of course," she said. "Have a seat."

I sat in front of her desk, facing the crystal ball. It always made me uncomfortable to look into the glass, since it blocked any magic that went near it, including my lie-sensing ability.

Her brow wrinkled as she leaned over the glass. "It's tricky, Blair. Your fate is clouded… I've always had trouble reading you. No doubt it's your fairy heritage… but I see a great choice will soon arrive for you. An important one which might have a ripple effect on everyone who comes into contact with you."

"Really?" My voice came out small. "Anything more specific?"

"Fairies are hard to read," she said. "If you wanted a stronger glimpse into the future, you'd need a Seeing Stone."

I flinched at the word. "Seeing Stone?"

"Yes," she said. "Granted, you'd have a battle and a half asking the regional witch council to let you borrow it, but it's as effective on fairies as it is on witches, unlike crystal balls."

Was that why my dad had wanted it so badly? *Was he looking into* my *future?* Or was he looking to learn the fate of the fairies in general? He must have been desperate, but then again, he'd been on the run for years at that point.

A fresh wave of despair hit me at the reminder that he didn't have the Pixie-Glass after all, so I had no way to talk to him and ask what he'd really wanted with the Seeing Stone. He wouldn't have risked his own safety for no reason, right? Yet the only people who might have the answers were those he'd stayed with while he'd been on the run, but I was pretty sure I'd already heard everything the elves were willing to tell me.

The fairies, though?

Conor Underwood. Perhaps I ought to press him for more information. He must know at least some of my family history, if he'd lived in hiding here in Fairy Falls for years.

Maybe he also knew what my dad had been looking for.

11

After leaving the seer's shop, I walked along the same route to Conor Underwood's house as I had before. Sky decided against coming with me, and I didn't particularly blame him for it, after his unfortunate encounter with the plants in the garden. To no surprise, I ended up lost in the woods for at least half an hour, and when I finally found my way to the right house, I found the fairy's cottage in exactly the same state as the last time I'd been here. I knocked on the door, which opened.

I looked at Conor for a long moment, unsure where to begin. I hadn't told him the Inquisitor was a fairy, though he already knew the hunters had arrested my dad. As for my mother, though? No way could I admit that my ancestors had probably driven his out of town. If I did, I'd lose any chance of ever getting his help or the other fairies' support. At the same time, though, maybe he could enlighten me on Mrs Dailey's odd alliance with the Inquisitor. There must be a way to bring up the subject without admitting my own connection to her coven. You'd think he would have heard about her attempted coup, even from here.

"You again," he said. "What is it this time?"

"I tried to speak to my dad using a Pixie-Glass," I began.

His eyes flashed with some emotion I couldn't read. "Is that so? You spoke to him?"

"No," I said. "Someone else had the glass instead. One of the Inquisitor's allies who's supposed to be under close watch in the Lancashire Prison for Paranormals has a Pixie-Glass. She… she's not my biggest fan."

"Is she a fairy?" he asked.

"Witch." I swallowed hard. "And I found out her ancestors were the ones who… who banished the fairies from the Falls."

"She *what?*"

His anger hit me like a whip, and an ominous rumble of thunder came from behind him. An instant later, the skies split, and rain pounded down on my head in a deluge which drenched me to the skin within seconds. I staggered back, wings beating fast to stop me from getting swept away in the storm. His magic was raw and terrifying, and I knew I never should have assumed him to be harmless.

"Calm down!" I yelped. "I just want to help you."

"I don't need your help," he said, his voice all but lost in the pounding rain and crackling thunder.

"But I need yours." I held my hands over my head in a futile attempt to shield myself. "You're the first fairy I've met who hasn't tried to kill me or recruit me to join the hunters, and I can't do this alone. I need to prove the

Inquisitor is a liar and that he arrested my dad illegally, but he has too many people on his side, including the witch whose ancestors banished the fairies. I'm not on her side. I just want to save my dad."

My voice broke on the last word, and I fought to hold back tears of frustration more than fear.

Gradually, the rain stopped. The wild wind halted a moment later, leaving me drenched and shivering but mercifully unhurt. My knees trembled. If the Inquisitor's fairy magic was even stronger than Conor's, how would I ever be able to thwart him?

"The Inquisitor worked with this witch," he said. "The man in charge of the hunters is allied with someone who drove the fairies from the Falls?"

"Yeah," I said. "But—*he's* a fairy. The Inquisitor is, I mean."

"A fairy?" He looked askance at me. "Who exactly is this Inquisitor?"

He didn't know? If he'd lived inside his glamoured fairyland for years, he'd certainly missed a lot, that was for sure.

"I wish I knew," I replied. "I mean, his name is Inquisitor Hare, but I'm guessing that wasn't his name when he lived with the fairies. If he ever did." I was babbling, but he'd frankly scared me half to death, and I wasn't sure I wanted to see him go head to head with the Inquisitor. Even if he stood a chance against him, their clashing magic might well wipe the whole town off the map.

Mrs Dailey's ancestors must have had an uncommon magical gift to drive the fairies out of town, though if they'd had other fairies on their side, it wouldn't have been impossible. That was the Inquisitor's goal, after all—to turn fairy against fairy, and paranormal against paranormal.

"This Inquisitor is a traitor to our kind," he said, his jaw tense and his eyes bright with anger. "The other fairies would never stand for such a betrayal."

"He's too powerful to overcome," I said. "And he has the support of everyone in the hunters because they think he's human. If I could find a way to publicly prove he isn't... is that possible?"

"Glamour always has a weak point," he said. "If you know where to look."

"I can't see through his glamour myself," I said. "Is there a way for me to get in touch with the other fairies? Maybe they can help expose his illusion."

"No," he said. "The fairies from the Courts are likely too scared to challenge him or are otherwise indifferent. As for us independent exiles, the witches drove us out of their world a long time ago." Sadness laced his voice.

"You aren't alone," I told him. "My friends are spreading the word among the other hunters that the Inquisitor is a fraud. We're going to expose him in front of the regional witch council, if we can."

"You can't," he insisted. "If he's been fooling everyone into believing he's human for years, he's been in his position too long not to have plans at the ready for this very scenario. If nobody knows who he truly is, his disguise must be faultless."

"Maybe, but I don't know what else to do," I said. "He's coming for me anyway. To recruit me. And I don't know what he'll do when I say no."

Conor's gaze sharpened. "He wants to recruit you? Are you going to refuse?"

"Of course I'll say no," I said. "He arrested my dad, and his hunters kept me from seeing my birth parents for my entire life. I'd have to be out of my mind to ever want to work for him. He didn't even tell me he was a fairy. I figured that out on my own."

"Then," he said, "I will endeavour to help you the best I can."

Gratitude flooded me, tempered by wariness. "Um, I think it's best to keep the storms to a minimum. Is there a way for you to contact the other fairies?"

"If you want my help," he said. "I might be able to contact the others, but I'd need a communication device."

"You mean a Pixie-Glass?"

Oh, no. Not this again. I'd barely got away with borrowing it the first time around.

"Yes, Blair," he said. "That's the only method I know of which would give me direct contact with the others."

"But… the person on the other side of the glass is the witch I was talking about earlier," I said. "The one whose ancestors drove your fellow fairies out of town. I don't know how to stop her from appearing every time I use the glass."

"Maybe I will speak to her myself," he growled. "I will make her glad to be behind bars."

"Um, she also has direct contact with the Inquisitor and his allies, so—"

"I thought you wanted to confront him," he said.

"I do, but not before I'm ready," I said. "Besides, the last thing we need to do is have him set Mrs Dailey free. She has mind-controlling powers. She also nearly wiped out my memories the last time we met face to face, and that's just one reason she's in jail."

"Is that so?" he said. "Regardless, if I'm to contact the other fairies, then I'll need the Pixie-Glass."

So be it. I should have known it wouldn't be easy to find his allies, but the notion of getting myself entangled in another of the Inquisitor's spells wasn't appealing. Would we be able to get away with borrowing the Pixie-Glass a second time? What if Nathan was the one who paid the price? Or one of his siblings? I couldn't protect everyone.

Then I'd have to go myself.

"All right," I said. "I'll come back later. With the Pixie-Glass."

When I reached the real-world part of the forest, my phone buzzed with a belated message from Nathan. *Where are you?*

I messaged him back asking to meet him near the edge of the forest, then set about finding my way out. When I did so, I found Nathan waiting for me on the path near the witches' area of town. "Steve is angry."

"Why?" I asked.

"He found out about my father's visit to the border," he said. "He's had me send out extra patrols to make sure he isn't still lurking around."

"Can't hurt," I said. "We're expecting the Inquisitor to show his face any day now, right?"

"Yes, but I'm not sure any more patrols will do any good. He still technically has the authority over them."

Unfortunately, he was probably right. "How's your sister doing?"

"Erin keeps updating me with details about the

hunters she's contacted," he said. "I'm free for now, anyway. Want to grab lunch somewhere?"

"Charms & Caffeine?" I suggested. "I'd pick the bookshop café, but I think I've seen enough of Vincent for one day." I still didn't know what to make of his words about my family earlier that morning, for that matter.

Nathan and I made our way to the coffee shop. Layla, Lizzie's sister, waved at us from behind the counter as we ordered coffee and sandwiches from a table by the window.

"Erin has been talking to the hunters, then?" I picked up my sandwich and bit into it.

"Yes, she's been going through her contacts," he said. "I hope she hasn't given too much away about our plan. I also hope she wasn't out in that thunderstorm."

My heart gave a lurch. "You saw the thunderstorm?"

"Sure," he said. "It'd have been difficult to miss it."

What? But I thought Conor's magic was confined to the weird illusory glamour world around his cottage. Had the whole town experienced a freakish mini lightning storm?

"The fairy caused the storm," I explained. "He didn't take it well when I told him Mrs Dailey was related to the same witches who drove the fairies out of town."

His brows rose. "You told him?"

"I didn't know how else to convince him I needed his help," I said. "At least we know he has powerful magic, though maybe not enough to give the Inquisitor a run for his money. I thought only the two of us could see the storm, though. We were inside the fairy's garden at the time."

"I definitely saw it," he said. "I don't know if anyone

else would have realised a fairy created the storm, but if there are any other fairies in the area...."

"Like the Inquisitor." Oh, no. "I told Conor Underwood about him, too, but he didn't know who he was, so I assume they weren't acquainted with one another before Conor went into hiding. Not that he can do anything, though. He says the rogue fairies are completely scattered and the only way to reach them is to use the Pixie-Glass to contact each of them. At least it sounds like Erin and Buck are making good progress."

"What's the plan for after they run out of hunters and ex-hunters to talk to?" he asked.

"I was going to make calls at work, but Veronica shut the office." I finished my sandwich and sipped from my coffee mug. "I still need to find Blythe, but I don't know where she's staying. Maybe Rebecca will know."

"She'll be out of school soon," he commented. "Did you tell the fairy you'd bring him the Pixie-Glass?"

"Yeah, but I don't know if we'll get away with taking it again," I admitted. "I'll speak to Blythe first. She deserves to know what her mother is up to. Whether she'll be interested to learn our family history or not... well. I can't say she'll thank me for it, but it has to be said."

"I'll see if I can contact Eric," he said. "To find out if the Inquisitor has given him any more instructions. Then I'll see if we can get the Pixie Glass again."

"Are you sure?" I said. "Last time was risky enough, and the Inquisitor definitely knows we took it. That's why he had Mrs Dailey waiting on the other side."

"We need all the allies we can get." He finished his coffee. "I have to go and check in with Steve. See you later?"

"Sure." I wrapped my arms around him as he stood up to leave. "I know it's a lot."

"Honestly, I think my family needs to know what the Inquisitor is, and as soon as possible," he said. "Everyone does. Maybe the other fairies can help unmask him. If he's been in disguise for so long that even the other fairies don't know who he really is, though…"

"I wouldn't say Conor Underwood has exactly been in contact with the outside world over the last few years." I drained the last few drops of coffee. "But yeah, we need to expose him."

I just hope we have enough strength between us to beat him.

After parting ways with Nathan, I walked to the local witch academy and waited outside the gates for the students to start leaving. Within half an hour or so, the bells rang, and groups of students began filing through the gates. Rebecca was easy enough to spot, her sceptre tucked under her arm and Toast padding along at her side. Her familiar meowed a greeting when he saw me.

"Blair." She walked up to me. "Is something wrong?"

"I'm looking for your sister." I crouched and stroked Toast on his head. "I need to talk to her, but I don't know where she's staying. I wondered if you did."

"Blythe?" she said. "Last I heard, she was renting a house down by the lake. I can come with you, if you like."

I shifted uncomfortably. Already, the other students were starting to stare at us, realising who I was.

"That's the fairy witch," said a girl in a carrying whisper. "Why's she with the Head Witch?"

"What are they plotting?" her friend whispered back.

"Maybe they're going to shut down the academy next."

I tuned out the voices and walked with Rebecca until we left the crowd behind. "What's with the rumours?"

"Sorry," she said. "I think Sammi overheard Madame Grey talking about all these coven meetings she's having and assumed we were involved."

Well, she's not wrong. "Oh. I guess I see why she'd think that."

"What's going on?" she asked. "Aren't you supposed to be at work?"

"My boss gave us the day off," I said. "Um, you can go home if you like. I just need a quick word with Blythe."

"You can't leave me out of this," she said. "I know something big is going on. The other kids at school do, too, and they keep asking me questions. Besides, I *am* Head Witch."

She wasn't wrong. More to the point, she'd likely be attending the meeting with the regional witch council next week, which meant the truth would come out sooner or later.

"It's about your mother," I said. "I spoke to her yesterday."

Fear flashed across her face. "How?"

"Don't worry, she's still in jail," I added hastily. "But she has contact with the outside world, which she shouldn't have. I need to talk to Blythe about that. I didn't want to upset you…"

"But you think she's coming back to town?" she said quietly.

"No." But my words rang hollow. "She's still safely behind bars, but the Inquisitor is working with her, and he's coming after me."

She halted at the street's end and pointed to a house

along a terraced row facing the lake. "Blythe's renting that house over there. I have to go home to Mrs Farringdon, but please tell me if she—she's coming back. I want to know the truth."

"I will," I promised. "I promise, though, the Inquisitor has never mentioned you. It's me he's after, and your mother won't be allowed to walk free. See you later, okay?"

As she departed, I knocked on the door of the house she'd pointed out. Nobody answered at first, so I hovered on the doorstep, taking in the view of the lake. It would be a pretty nice place for a holiday, if you discounted the random fairy storms and the possible impending visit from the hunters. I scanned the lake's rippling surface and spotted Blythe walking along the shore. Leaving the cottage behind, I headed in her direction.

She rolled her eyes when she saw me. "I figured you'd track me down."

"I came to the house, but you weren't there," I said.

"Who told you... right, Rebecca did." She scowled. "Where do I have to go to get some peace from you?"

"Hey, I've hardly spoken to you in weeks," I said indignantly.

She gave another eye-roll. "I'm guessing that freak thunderstorm earlier was your work?"

Oops. "Nope. That was the person whose address you gave me. He's a fairy, and let's just say he doesn't like your mother."

"Who does?" she said. "I saw you wandering around up at the other end of the lake the other day, too. I take it you were meeting with another dubious ally?"

"Nathan's father," I admitted. "I tried to convince him

the Inquisitor is a liar and a fraud. Not sure if I got through to him, but if I tell as many of the hunters as possible that their leader's a fraud, I figured it'd weaken his hold on them."

"I thought your plan was to speak to your dad," she said.

"Didn't quite work out," I said. "Your mother got in the way. She has the only Pixie-Glass in the LPFP."

She swore. "Of course she does. So you drew *her* attention."

"She was waiting for me, Blythe. She and the Inquisitor expected me to make contact. I was telling your sister—"

"You *told* my sister our mother is back to her scheming ways?" Blythe interjected. "What's wrong with you?"

"She's Head Witch, Blythe," I said. "It's unfair to keep her in the dark, besides."

"She's a kid. Are you determined to mess up her life?"

"Your mother already tried to do that already, and she deserves to know," I said. "Speaking of whom, Mrs Dailey told me our ancestors were once the ruling coven here in Fairy Falls."

"So?" she said. "She told me that when I was five. Is it really news to you?"

"Did she tell you it was our ancestors who drove the fairies out of town centuries ago, too?" I asked.

Blythe's eyes widened. "What?"

"Didn't think so," I said. "Our ancestors are the reason the fairies left the Falls. I'm not sure why the Inquisitor still wants me to work for him anyway, but the original coven who drove the fairies out of town..."

"They were our predecessors," Blythe finished, her

voice oddly hushed. "I—I'm surprised she didn't *tell* me. Maybe she thought it'd make me less supportive of her plan to replace the covens with the hunters."

"I guess that's why she hated my mum and dad so much, too," I added.

"You're telling me," she said. "Does knowing the truth really give you any more of an advantage over the hunters, though? They're still winning."

"The Inquisitor is breaking the law by giving Mrs Dailey more freedom than she's entitled to," I said. "He's also lying to his fellow hunters about who he really is. I'm sure the reason he and Mrs Dailey are allies is because of their history with the fairies. If it all comes out in the open, then the hunters' trust in him will be shaken."

"You think you can expose him?" she said in sceptical tones. "You're not meeting him face to face, are you?"

"He invited me to meet with him," I said. "He knew I'd try to contact my dad and end up facing your mother instead, so it's safe to say he already knows what I'm going to do before even *I* do. Maybe *he* has a crystal ball."

Or a Seeing Stone.

Her jaw tensed. "Whatever the case, you don't need to drag my sister into this mess."

"She already has an invitation to the meeting with the regional witch coven next week," I pointed out. "Unless Madame Grey manages to get her out of it, she's going to be forced to attend the meeting of the regional witch council along with the Inquisitor's personal ambassador. Besides, the Inquisitor likes your mother. He won't harm Rebecca."

"He'll exploit her," she said. "You can't deny it."

"I think he's more concerned with exploiting *me,*

unless he sent her an invitation to work for the hunters, too."

"He won't have, because she's only eleven," she said. "Doesn't mean he won't be waiting to recruit her at graduation from the academy."

"Assuming he's still the leader of the hunters by then."

"You're expecting too much to come of this little plan of yours," she said. "You can't depose someone who's led the hunters since we were little kids. He's way too powerful. You're deluding yourself if you think otherwise, Blair."

"Maybe," I said, "but I'm not alone."

That had always been the difference between the two of us. Blythe believed she was on her own, and that everyone else was out to get her. I couldn't really blame her, given her upbringing, but I would never leave Rebecca to face the hunters alone.

Blythe's brows rose at something behind me. "Maybe not."

I spun around in time to see Nathan approaching. Fast. *What happened?*

Nathan halted in front of me. "He's here, Blair. The Inquisitor. He's ready to talk to you."

12

---

he Inquisitor. He'd finally shown up in person.… and I wasn't ready. Not that I'd ever expected to be. Even though I'd only set eyes on him once before, his face had haunted my dreams on a regular basis since that day, and I'd known we'd have a reckoning from the moment I'd learned he wasn't human but a fairy. Like me, and yet nothing like me.

"Where does he want to meet me?" I asked Nathan, the merest tremor creeping into my voice.

"The witches' place," he said. "Alone."

All right. It wouldn't be like our last meeting, where all the other witches had been present, too, but what had I expected? He must know exactly what I was up to. The fact that he'd had Mrs Dailey waiting on the other side of the Pixie-Glass was proof of that.

Didn't mean I had the faintest idea what his angle would be this time around. He must know I'd all but refused his offer of employment already, but he'd come to Fairy Falls in person for a reason.

Nathan walked with me to the witches' headquarters. My hands shook at my sides, and I didn't dare voice my terror in case it made Nathan intervene on my behalf and end up becoming a target, too. He embraced me briefly outside the doors, and then let go with a whispered, "Good luck, Blair."

Drawing in a breath, I walked in, noting that the door to Rita's classroom was slightly ajar. I hoped Rebecca had gone straight home without coming here and setting eyes on the Inquisitor. Facing him alone was hard enough.

I drew in a breath, then walked into the coven meeting room. The Inquisitor sat alone at the end of the long table. No other witches were in sight, not even Madame Grey. What had he done, dismissed them from their own meeting room? Or used his magic? It was anyone's guess, but few would dare say no to him. Even the coven who ruled this town.

He watched me come in, a calculating expression on his face, and all thoughts of resistance fled my mind. I hadn't set eyes on him in long enough to forget the way his pressed suit contrasted the rugged clothing preferred by the other hunters, while his eyes were as dark as pitch. The instant he looked at me, blank walls filled my vision in place of my usual paranormal-sensing ability, and I fought the urge to back out of the room.

The Inquisitor looked at me like an animal watching its prey. If I had to guess what type of paranormal he was, I would have guessed a shifter and not a fairy, but only a powerful fairy like him had total immunity to my abilities.

"Blair Wilkes," he said. "Or should I call you Briar Wildflower?"

The sound of my mother's chosen name for me coming from his mouth unlocked my frozen limbs, and my hands shook as much in anger as in fear. "Call me Blair, please."

"Of course." He gestured to the table. "Do take a seat, will you?"

My heart lurched against my ribs as I approached the table and sat down opposite him. "Don't you want to talk to the other witches?"

"I believe you and I have important matters to discuss first." He leaned forwards. "Starting with your feeble attempts to recruit my fellow hunters."

I tensed. "If you mean Erin and Buck, they already planned to leave the hunters ages ago. Their choice had nothing to do with me."

"I might believe you," he said, "if not for the recent reports I've had from people who've received phone calls from the pair of them in the last day."

Of course he'd been monitoring his fellow hunters' phones. That figured.

"I wasn't involved," I said, truthfully enough. It wasn't like I'd made any calls myself, after all. "Maybe you should have been honest with them from the start."

"Most people don't have the ability to sense lies, Blair," he said. "Besides, when you have a job as important as leading the paranormal hunters, you must know that it's essential to project a certain image."

"Because a lot of them don't like paranormals," I said. "Except that's not what you told me when you tried to recruit me the first time around, is it? You told me the hunters *do* recruit from among paranormal communities."

"It matters very little to me who my hunters are, as long as they do a good job," he said. "You could have been an asset, Blair."

"I thought you *still* wanted to recruit me," I said. "Despite the fact that you jailed my father, and you're allowing Mrs Dailey freedom to contact the outside world despite her trying to wipe my memories and hurt my friends."

"Life is full of difficult decisions, Blair," he said. "If you and Mrs Dailey got to know one another, you might find you have much in common. Like her daughter."

Did he mean Blythe or Rebecca? Protectiveness towards the young Head Witch surged within me. "I doubt it. The only thing we have in common is that we're distantly related. She hates *both* sides of my family. With good reason. I bet she was really mad when my mother chose the fairies over her, though I'd have done the same."

"I don't doubt you would have, Blair, but Tanith Wildflower was well aware of the fairies' hatred of one another when she chose to pursue your father. I believe it was a game to her, to strengthen the already existing divisions between them and convince your father to leave the others."

Anger clenched around my heart. "You're wrong."

He *was* wrong. My parents had loved one another, and he and the other hunters had driven them apart. I would never forgive him. Never.

"And how would you know that, Blair?" he said.

"For a start, I've spoken to my mother myself," I said. "You can't speak for her, and you have no idea who she was or what she stood for."

"How..." He broke off. "Ah. The Head Witch won over

the sceptre on Samhain, so she would have had the opportunity to use its magic for you. I have to confess, none of us predicted that particular turn of events, even with a Seeing Stone."

His words reverberated in my skull. He'd even managed to guess that Rebecca and I had used the sceptre to summon the ghost of my mother last year when he'd been nowhere near us at the time. Was there anything he *didn't* know?

"When did this thing with Mrs Dailey start, then?" I said recklessly. "Before or after she tried to wipe out my memories and attacked me? Because I'd say I have good reason to be concerned about your motives in trying to recruit me, considering how much freedom you've given her."

"I believe Mrs Dailey regrets what she did to you, Blair," he said. "I meant it when I said you could be an asset to the hunters, and if you choose to join us, you will gain everything you desire."

"You don't know anything about what I want," I said. "I am nothing like Mrs Dailey, and neither was my mother."

"Oh, certain traits run in the family," he said. "I've met enough of your witch relatives, Blair, and they share a certain rebelliousness. Some are more righteous than others, while some are more easily led. I've been interested to see which way you would turn as your powers developed."

A wave of dizziness washed over me at the meaning underlying his words. "You mean my ancestors. The original Wildflower Coven. The ones who drove off the fairies."

"The very same," he said. "I think we are better off

living apart, personally. The fairies have no place among ordinary humans."

"You *lead the hunters.*" I fought to keep my temper under control. "You spend every day among humans, pretending to be one of them. Do you even hear yourself right now?"

"Yes," he said. "I do. There are certain sacrifices one must make for power, for both fairies and humans. Once I'd finished competing over crowns, I had new ambitions to realise."

"Crowns?" I echoed. "What does that mean? Does it have to do with my dad being a prince?"

"Among our kind, it's hardly an achievement," he said. "There are many princes and princesses, and one tires of their endless games. I found the human realm more suited to my ambitions."

"Did that include driving away the other fairies?" I said.

"The other exiled fairies have little power of their own," he said. "Driving them off was a simple matter, and a necessary one. They would have opposed my rule over the hunters, and the local covens were more than happy to help me achieve my goal."

My throat went dry. "You're talking like you were there. In person."

"You know true fairies are immortal, Blair," he said. "I have been here a very long time."

He's as old as Vincent. Maybe older. And yet he didn't look a day over forty. A chill raced down my back. Maybe that's why he'd always struck me as so dangerous. He was centuries older than I was, and he'd outlive me a thousand times over. He'd been here in Fairy Falls, spreading his poisonous influence over the covens, from the very start. Did Mrs Dailey know she worked with the very same man who'd allied with her ancestors to drive out the fairies? Did she care?

"You already have total control over the hunters," I said. "Why do you need to control me, then? You already have what you want."

"You're too disruptive to leave to your own devices," he said. "Especially with your recent actions."

"Recruiting me won't stop anyone from opposing you," I said. "People don't need my encouragement to leave the hunters, now your façade is collapsing. You didn't manage to drive off *all* the fairies. Some of them remember. One even tried to kill *me* over it, believing my father betrayed them. You left so much damage behind you that it even dragged me into it—a normal, from the normal world. Was that what you intended?"

He stared at me for a moment. "You're certainly more outspoken than the first time we met, Blair, but you seem to be unaware of the power I hold here in Fairy Falls. I remember when this town was nothing more than a smudge on the lakeside. I was here when it rose, and I can see to it that it disappears from the map once again if necessary."

Dread gripped me. He was old enough to remember everything, from the founding of Fairy Falls to his fellow fairies being driven out of town. Even the rise of the hunters. He'd been involved with them from their inception, yet the other hunters would have no idea. He was too clever, and he'd hidden his tracks well. Maybe I did have the courage to stand up to him, but he still held my father's fate in his hands. The town's, too.

"How many years did it take you to find my dad and have him jailed?" I said. "He was on the run for years, yet you never caught him until you pinned a theft on him and had him arrested. Are you sure you weren't too afraid to stand up to him in person?"

"You seem to be mistaken on the matter of your father's innocence," he said. "He wasn't framed. That wasn't necessary. He sealed his own fate when he took the Seeing Stone, Blair, and I am not lying."

My hands clenched under the table. *So it's true? He really did steal the Seeing Stone?*

Yet he must have had good reason, and it didn't merit the punishment he'd been charged with.

"He was jailed for life, and yet other people who committed the same crime were set free," I pointed out. "You can't pretend that there wasn't manipulation involved in his sentence."

"Your father's case was different because the Seeing Stone is still missing," he said. "In fact, we suspect your father alone knows where it is, yet he refuses to divulge any details no matter how many times we have interrogated him. Never call me too harsh, Blair… I could have done much worse than jail him."

I sat rigid in my seat. Deep down, part of me had always assumed my dad had been framed, or at the very least, set up, but if the Seeing Stone was *still* missing, years later… why would my dad have refused to tell the hunters where it was? It wasn't like I could tell if the Inquisitor was lying, yet he must know I'd be able to confirm with the regional witch council if he spoke true. If the Seeing Stone truly remained missing… then my last chance to get my dad off the hook had gone up in smoke.

"So," he went on, "I'm sure you can convince him to tell you where it is. I'd no doubt he would tell his only daughter the truth. If you then give the details to me, then we'll put this matter behind us."

My throat closed up. "I can't—I can't know where it is. He never told me anything even when we were in contact. He knew you were watching him."

"Oh, I'm sure he'll willingly tell you anything in a face-to-face conversation," he said. "Which you should be able to arrange."

The Pixie-Glass. "I thought his privileges had been taken away."

"I would be glad to make an exception in this case, Blair."

I didn't doubt it. If I used the Pixie-Glass to talk to my dad, then… then I'd be able to ask him to tell me where the Seeing Stone was. After that, the Inquisitor would have no choice but to let him go.

There must be a catch somewhere. The Inquisitor wasn't even pretending not to be manipulating me, but the idea of my dad finally being granted freedom was hard to resist.

"Do you expect him to tell me where the Seeing Stone is, knowing you're listening to our conversation?" I queried.

"Of course not," he said, an impatient bite to his voice. "I would give you the privacy you wanted for your conversation. You'll be free to catch up on the years you've missed together to your heart's content before you ask him where he hid the Seeing Stone."

"Then..." I looked away from his flat black eyes. "Then you want me to tell you where it is."

"Exactly," he said. "I'll send my people to retrieve the Seeing Stone and we'll process your father's papers immediately."

Too good to be true. He wouldn't just let my dad walk away free. Even if I had to steal the Pixie-Glass again, there must be a reason my dad had hidden the Seeing Stone. It belonged to the witches, not the hunters, for a start. Yet how could I tell truth from lie with my powers masked by the Inquisitor's overwhelming glamour?

There was also Conor Underwood to consider, too. He'd wanted to use the Pixie-Glass to contact the other fairies, and if I took it to him first, I might be able to gather more fairies to help back me up. But there was no *time.* The Inquisitor had already messed up my plans thoroughly, and I doubted he'd be leaving town before I contacted my dad.

"What happens if I fail?" I asked. "I mean, if he doesn't tell me where the Seeing Stone is... or if I fail to get my hands on the Pixie-Glass?"

"The catch?" he said. "If you were to fail, then I will contact your supervisor... Veronica, isn't it? I'll explain that you are to quit working for Eldritch & Co immediately and come and work for the paranormal hunters. Your lie-sensing power will be an asset to us, as will your ability to see through illusions. I'm sure you'll have no trouble tracking down your fellow rogue fairies."

His words hit my heart like the blows of a hammer.

He'd take away my job, my allies, and I'd bet if I moved to the hunters' base, I'd never see any of them again.

"If you succeed, of course," he said, "you won't have to worry about a thing."

"Why do you want the Seeing Stone?" I whispered.

"Because it is ours," he said. "Not your father's, and not the witches'."

He thought the hunters owned the Seeing Stone? What would the regional witch council make of that?

"I will wait for you," he told me. "I'll give you enough time to retrieve the Pixie-Glass and prepare, while we inform your father of the recent turn of events. Tonight, I'd advise you to say your goodbyes to your friends in case the worst should happen. Then tomorrow morning at nine, your father will be ready to talk to you. If you fail to contact him, then his sentence will become final, while if you succeed, it's on you to convince him to tell you the location of the Seeing Stone. I think that's fair, isn't it, Blair?"

"Does that mean…" I felt the last threads of hope slipping through my fingers. "Does that mean if he tells me where the Seeing Stone is, you'll let him go? There and then?"

"Of course," he said. "You'll be reunited at last, Blair. Isn't that what you wanted?"

Reunited… but free in the knowledge that the Inquisitor would be unopposed, and I'd given up my home and my life for his freedom. My father would never want that.

Yet I'd have to make that choice, or else lose my job, my allies, and everything I'd gained since I'd moved to Fairy Falls.

I rose to my feet and left the room, my eyes pricking with tears, my head pounding. How was I supposed to make this decision? Either way, someone I loved would suffer. Either way, the hunters would win.

Inquisitor Hare was blackmailing me... and I wasn't sure I had any resistance left in me to beat him.

13

"I have until nine tomorrow," I told Nathan. "Then I speak to my dad, and either he tells me where the Seeing Stone is or not. If I don't contact him, I'll never see him again. If he doesn't tell me, I have to join the hunters."

Nathan sucked in a breath. "That's blackmail."

"Of course it's blackmail, but what am I supposed to do?" I said. "For all I know, this Seeing Stone isn't really hidden at all. I don't know why my dad would hide it and refuse to tell anyone, when divulging its location would win him his freedom back."

"You're right—it doesn't add up," he said. "You can't sense when the Inquisitor is lying, can you?"

"Unfortunately not," I replied. "It's frustrating, because I know he's manipulating me, but I can't *prove* it. All I can do is speak to my dad instead, which means I have to borrow the Pixie-Glass again. I suppose we could simplify things and tell Eric that the Inquisitor wants me to use the glass in the hopes that he'll hand it over without us needing to pull off another stealth mission. If he'd believe us, that is."

His expression darkened. "I haven't heard from Eric since we last took the Pixie-Glass. It's entirely possible he noticed its absence, but if Erin has told him the truth about the Inquisitor's identity, he might have formed his own opinion."

"You said that's unlikely, though," I said. "It would be nice to imagine he'd take our side, but even if he believes me, is he really going to stand up against the Inquisitor? He's too powerful and influential for anyone to take the risk. I totally screwed this up."

"Blair, don't panic," said Nathan. "I'll call Eric and see if I can persuade him to hand over the glass. If not, we'll repeat the same plan we used yesterday. We can get the Pixie-Glass by the morning, no problem."

"That's the easy bit." I sighed. "Conor wanted me to bring him the Pixie-Glass, too, and at this point, getting in contact with the other fairies is my only backup plan. Either way, though, we need that glass."

If I went to Eric's house in person, I'd be more likely to be caught, since it was my second time taking the risk within the space of two days. Besides, for all I knew, the Inquisitor had warned his assistant we were coming. It wouldn't surprise me. Yet he *wanted* me to have the glass, right?

Nathan and I neared my house, and my heart sank at the notion of telling the others how much trouble I'd ended up in.

"I have to warn Alissa," I said to him. "I suppose Madame Grey might be willing to help us out, but I wouldn't blame her if she isn't. I shouldn't have provoked the Inquisitor."

While he'd always had his eye on Fairy Falls, it was hard not to believe I was to blame for him choosing this moment to come here and deliver an ultimatum.

"Blair." Nathan drew me into his arms. "We'll get through this. I'll call my brother. I also have to check in with Steve, who wants an explanation about the Inquisitor's presence in town—"

"Of course he does." I groaned. "I suppose if Steve locked me in jail, it couldn't be much worse than going to work for the Inquisitor full-time."

Yet despite the Inquisitor's threats, my desire to speak to my dad burned under my skin, undaunted. Even if he didn't tell me where the Seeing Stone was, even if he didn't *know* where it was—I had to try, for my dad's sake… and for my mum's, and everyone else in town who might end up locked in the darkness if they had their way.

Nathan and I parted ways outside my house, where I walked into the garden and almost collided with Vincent the vampire.

"Whoa." I caught my balance against the fence, almost falling into the bed of fairy-proof flowers. *That was a close one.* "What are you doing here?"

"I had an inkling you were in some trouble again, Blair." He stepped aside and Sky peered out from behind his leg. The little cat must have called him here for another chat.

"I guess you heard the Inquisitor is in town," I said. "He's blackmailing me into finding something my dad stole and hid somewhere before he was jailed. I assume you know what a Seeing Stone is, but my dad took it from the regional witch coven. I don't know why the Inquisitor thinks my dad would have hidden it instead of handing it over when he was arrested, but if you have any idea where he might have put it…"

"I'm afraid I don't, Blair," said the vampire. "If your father truly hid this Seeing Stone, then he might not even have hidden it in Fairy Falls."

"The Inquisitor seemed certain I'd be able to find it," I said. "But he could easily be lying. I doubt he'll leave town until I give him what he wants. So… I guess if you want to warn the other vampires and take off, I wouldn't blame you for it."

"Interesting," he said. "I assume that's why Madame Grey has been contacting the regional witch council representatives with an urgent request to come to town as soon as possible."

"She has?" I said, disarmed. "I guess that was before the Inquisitor derailed all our plans by showing up without warning. It won't make any difference if the witch council is here, though. The hunters *are* the authority, or so they keep reminding me."

"Yes, with the permission of the covens," he said. "That didn't used to be the case. I believe the law was set up back when the hunters and the witches were more closely aligned."

"When the Inquisitor and the covens conspired to drive all the other fairies out of town and made some kind of deal with one another," I surmised. "My ancestors were tied up with the hunters from the beginning. Once they'd driven off the fairies, they wanted to ensure they never came back… not the fairies they didn't like, anyway. And they wanted to ensure no other paranormals gained the upper hand, either."

"I imagine you're right, Blair," Vincent said.

"Did *you* know the Inquisitor and my ancestors worked hand in hand to expel the fairies from the Falls?" I said. "I assume you did."

"Would you have wanted to know your distant ancestors were once allied with your enemy?" he said. "You already knew Blythe's mother was his ally, and I assumed that would have been enough for you to put two and two together."

"There's no need to rub it in," I said to the vampire. "Might have escaped your attention, but I'm not in the mood. I have less than twenty-four hours to find a way out of this mess, or else the town ends up with the hunters in charge and I'm forced to *work* for them."

"It's certainly a troublesome situation," he said.

"How are you so calm?" I said. "You can read minds, but you can't see the future. I mean, I assume not."

"No, vampires and crystal balls don't generally go together," he said. "However, I confess that I saw a situation like this coming from the time of your first meeting with the Inquisitor."

"Then you must have some idea of how to show everyone that he's a liar and a manipulator," I said. "Can't you read his mind?"

"I cannot, and I have no authority over him."

I wanted to scream. "Then I guess this is it. I'm off to commit a robbery, and by tomorrow morning at the latest, either the hunters will be in charge of town or you'll never see me again."

"Miaow," Sky said from beside me.

"Your cat begs to differ," said Vincent.

"Sky didn't see the Inquisitor." I crouched down beside him. "I'm sorry, Sky. I doubt they'll let me bring you with me to work for the hunters. I don't see them being fans of fairy cats there."

"MIAOW." He swiped me with a claw. I recoiled when the giant form of Sky the monster appeared, so suddenly that I overbalanced and fell into the bushes.

"Ah!" I sprang upward, too late. The smell of the fairy-proofed flowers filled my nostrils, and to my horror, glittering sores began to pop up on my arms. "Sky!"

"You do have a knack for making an unfortunate situation worse, Blair," said Vincent, amusement glittering in his eyes.

"At least I know the house is still fairy-proofed." I rubbed my arm. "I suppose if I covered myself in flowers, the Inquisitor wouldn't be able to take me away."

"I'd advise you not to do that, Blair," said Vincent. "Let me know if you need the assistance of a mind-reader, won't you?"

And with one step, he was gone, vanishing from sight like only a vampire could.

"That vampire." I shook my head, wincing as the rash spread over my hands and up my arms. Turning around, I saw Alissa and Nina watching from the doorway. "How much did you hear?"

"Enough." Alissa stepped towards me. "Come on, I'll get rid of that rash. You can fill me on the rest inside the flat, okay?"

I followed her and Nina into my flat, and while Alissa brewed an antidote to the rash, I explained everything to both of them. There was no point in keeping any secrets. The whole town would know soon enough.

Nina listened with rapt attention and dawning horror, not having heard the truth about the Inquisitor's identity or my parents' fates before. "He *killed* your mother?"

"I doubt he did it himself," I said. "He might have given the order, but even a vampire couldn't wring the truth from him. As for my dad…"

"He'll be set free tomorrow." Alissa approached with the antidote in hand. "If you give the Inquisitor the Seeing Stone."

I took the antidote from her and drank it. "I doubt it'll be that straightforward. We still don't have the Pixie-Glass, for a start."

A cooling sensation spread down my chest to my limbs. The itching faded from my arms, and the rash gradually began to disappear.

"You need another transportation spell," she said. "It shouldn't matter as much if we're caught—"

"I didn't say 'we'," I said. "I'm the one who got myself into this mess. I'll go alone, using my wand to get in and out—"

"Miaow," Sky interrupted.

"I think he's volunteering to go with you," said Alissa. "You can at least take Sky if you want to do this alone, right?"

"Look, it doesn't matter either way," I said. "None of this makes any difference. If I succeed, the hunters will take power in Fairy Falls and dismiss the covens. And if I fail, I'll have to leave myself. No matter what the outcome, the fairies will never feel safe to come back here."

She pursed her lips. "I'll prepare the invisibility potions again. The transportation spell, too."

"Thanks," I said distractedly. "I don't know what to do. I mean, aside from panic. I have until morning to sort out this mess, and even if I do, I'm not sure it'll be enough."

Sky meowed loudly at me, but even he couldn't quell the sense of impending doom hanging over my shoulders. I couldn't settle, and since my focus levels were nowhere near good enough to help Alissa with the potion, I paced in circles around the room until an idea hit me like a bolt of fairy-magic induced lightning. Dislodging the pixie from one of his hiding spots above the coat rack, I grabbed my coat and made for the door.

"Blair, where are you going?" asked Alissa.

"To see my boss," I said. "It's not fair to leave town without warning her. Besides, she might know more about the Seeing Stone that I haven't thought of yet. Maybe we can find it ourselves, and then my dad won't have to get involved and I can return it to the hunters before the deadline."

Regardless, the hunters would still win. The Inquisitor would be less inclined to set my dad free, while he would still have control over my life and my future. Unless I figured out how to thwart him first.

I swiftly walked out the flat and through the town until I reached Dritch & Co's office. While none of my co-workers were in, of course, the automatic doors slid open to reveal the reception area. Relief hit me when I saw the glow of a light under Veronica's office door. Bracing myself, I skirted Callie's unoccupied desk and knocked.

"Yes?" said Veronica.

"It's me." I pushed open the door to her office, and at

the sight of the gleaming flowers, a lump filled my throat and my eyes watered. I sank onto the tree stump, and, holding back tears, told her about my meeting with the Inquisitor.

"Oh, Blair." Veronica rose to her feet and hugged me. I startled in surprise at the gesture. It was the most affection I'd ever received from my absentminded boss in the months I'd worked here. "Don't give in to the hunters."

"I don't have much choice." I fumbled in my pocket for a tissue and blew my nose. "The Seeing Stone… is there the slightest chance he was lying about it still being missing?"

She returned to her desk. "I'm afraid not. I called the regional witch coven and asked them about the theft of the stone myself, and there's no doubt it has been missing for as long as your father has been jailed."

My last hope evaporated. "Why would he have hidden it? Did he see the future—did he see *me?*" The words choked me. If my father had seen a vision of me being hauled off by the hunters and had hoped to change my fate by hiding the stone, then it had made no difference in the end. Yet it was no wonder he'd been reluctant to let me be part of the paranormal world, if he'd sacrificed his freedom for mine.

Veronica was silent for a moment. "I can only guess what your father saw in the Seeing Stone, but like crystal balls, its visions are not fixed in place. As for why he might have hidden the stone, I doubt it was due to anything he saw inside the glass. Why does the Inquisitor want it?"

I wiped my eyes on my sleeve. "I don't know, but if my

dad wanted to keep the stone hidden, then why not just give it back to the witches? I thought they owned it."

"The regional witch coven are the official owners, yes," she said.

"But the Inquisitor still has influence over them," I said slowly. "I know it's a stretch, but what if my dad was framed all along and someone else hid it? Or he hid the Seeing Stone himself, but because he thought the hunters had control over the regional witch coven and didn't want them to have it?"

"Perhaps he did, but you'd need proof, Blair," she said. "You'd also need to find the Seeing Stone yourself."

"I don't even know what the Seeing Stone looks like," I said.

"It resembles a crystal ball, but jet black in colour," she said. "And you may be able to find where your father put it without the need to ask him. You know where he and your mother lived during their brief time together, do you not?"

I frowned. "What? I don't know where he lived."

Or did I? An image entered my mind. The forest... and mother's old cottage, overgrown and abandoned.

"Think, Blair," she said. "I know where you went at Samhain."

"You think he might have put the Seeing Stone at my mum's old house?" I frowned. "I mean, it's possible. I didn't see any signs of a crystal ball last time I went there, but I wasn't on the lookout for anything in particular. Suppose it's worth a shot."

"Yes, and I will talk to Madame Grey about the regional witch council," she said. "I think I have an idea."

"What idea?" I said, but she'd already picked up the phone and dialled.

Whatever plan Veronica had come up with, I'd have to wait until later to find out. I rose to my feet and left the office, finding Sky sitting outside the door. Checking up on me, I guessed. I crouched down and gave him a stroke.

"C'mon, Sky," I said. "Let's go to my mum's old house."

———

Sky padded alongside me through the woods, around the outskirts of the elves' territory. Even with the background noise of the town's citizens heading home from work, silence folded over our heads almost instantly as we turned off the path and came to the cottage which had once been my mum's old house.

The sun had begun to set, washing the tips of the trees as I walked into the garden. The house itself looked as unsteady as ever with its roof tiles missing and the door sagging in its frame. The fence had half-collapsed, giving way to nature as the forest and garden merged at the back. Cobwebs cloaked the windows, obscuring the view inside, but I didn't see any sign of a jet-black crystal ball from here. If it was anywhere at all, it must be hidden inside the house.

I opened the gate and stepped into the garden, breathing in the smell of the herbs my mother had once grown. Then I carefully pushed open the door to the house and entered the dust-strewn hallway. The smell of must and mould caught in my nostrils, making me cough, and the unsteady-looking floorboards made me reluctant to climb the stair. Still, it wasn't like I didn't have wings, so I brought them out with a snap of my fingers.

Downstairs, most traces of personality had been removed or smothered in a layer of dust. With no signs of the Seeing Stone in sight, I flew upstairs and peered into each room. Yet no matter how hard I looked, I found no traces of a jet-black crystal ball.

As I returned to the landing, the sound of footsteps came from downstairs. My spine stiffened at the unmistakeable human sound. Had I been followed? I snapped my fingers to turn into my human form again, and trod carefully downstairs, Sky padding protectively at my side.

I reached the hall and found myself nose to nose with none other than Mr Harker. Of all the people I'd expected to see, Nathan's father was bottom of the list. Had he come to gloat at me, and in my mum's old house of all places?

Disbelief flooded away the remaining traces of my fear of him, mostly evaporated in the wake of the Inquisitor's ultimatum. "What do you want?"

"To speak to you," he said. "This was your mother's house."

"Yes, it was." I gave him a wary look. "Why are you here?"

"You're looking for something, aren't you?" he said. "If you are, it's probably gone. The house was thoroughly searched after your mother's departure."

"By the hunters." My hands clenched. "They took her possessions. They took away her only chance to ever see her daughter. And yet you still worked with them. You knew that, and you still..." I trailed off, rage choking my breath.

He ignored my words. "I expected my son to be with you."

"He's busy helping the police to prepare for your boss to attempt to oust the covens and take over the town," I told him. "Nathan has spent the better part of the last year setting up the town's new security force, and thanks to the Inquisitor, it's all for nothing."

"The Inquisitor first joined the hunters before you were born," he said. "He then became leader twenty years ago."

"What's your point?"

"I'm going to ignore your lack of manners and repeat my words," he said. "Inquisitor Hare joined the hunters about three decades ago. Before then, he didn't exist, according to any records. However... I found this."

He held up a photo. An old one, judging by the black and white colouring and the faded edges. A group of smudged faces blurred together until I reached the one in the centre, which I knew as well as I knew my own.

The Inquisitor. Yet despite the ancient photo, he looked the exact same as he did now.

"Why are you showing me this?" I said. "I don't understand."

"This photo is almost a hundred years old," he said. "I doubt Inquisitor Hare knows it exists."

"So it proves he's an immortal?" I said. "Would the other hunters believe you if you told them? They've worshipped him for years. Besides, he could claim the guy in the picture is just a relative or an ancestor or something. It's not like there's any more proof."

"Take the photo." He all but shoved it into my hand.

"Along with the other proof you have, it might be enough."

I don't have any other proof. Yet his gesture knocked me off-balance. Had my words actually got through to him? It seemed surreal, and yet the photo was real enough. And according to my lie-sensing talent, he'd been truthful.

"I asked my son to bring you the Pixie-Glass," he said. "It should be here within the hour."

As I gaped after him, he turned around and left me standing there in the hallway. Sky brushed against my leg, drawing my attention back to the present.

"What in the world was that about, Sky?" I murmured.

"Miaow," he replied, which probably meant, *I've no idea.*

"Your guess is as good as mine." I pocketed the photo, utterly bewildered at Mr Harker's change of heart.

Thanks to him, we'd be able to get the Pixie-Glass without any need for breaking and entering… which gave us until morning to figure out another way to use it to our advantage without giving in to the Inquisitor's whims. The Seeing Stone wasn't in the cottage, though, so my dad must have stashed it somewhere else, assuming the hunters hadn't already taken it back.

Maybe Conor Underwood knew. With the glass, I'd be able to ask him to contact the other fairies, since my dad wouldn't be allowed to speak to me until nine tomorrow morning. That didn't mean I was keen on the idea of potentially listening to Mrs Dailey gloat at me again. Conor had been certain he'd be able to use the glass without any issues, but a nagging doubt remained within me. I never had confirmed Conor was unequivocally an ally, or how he'd avoided the hunters for so long.

Wait. The Inquisitor had said the other exiled fairies had no magic. But Conor clearly *did* have magic, because his entire house was covered in glamour. His hiding place hadn't come out of nowhere, while the storm he'd conjured up spoke of a talent which I had a hard time believing the Inquisitor wouldn't have picked up on.

What if my only fairy ally was anything but? Before I gave him the Pixie-Glass, I needed to know if he was truly on my side.

14

I headed to the fairy's house, with Sky at my side. I didn't think the old photograph would count as evidence against the Inquisitor on its own, but on top of more proof, maybe it would be worth something. I was too weirded out by the fact that Nathan's father of all people had been the one to give it to me to really think about much else, but *if the Inquisitor unleashed all his power, I still couldn't count on them to stand beside me.*

I reached Conor Underwood's house, and Sky waited at the gate as I entered the garden and walked to the door.

The fairy answered at the first knock. "You again?"

"The Inquisitor is in town," I told him. "He's here. So are the hunters."

His gaze slid from me to Sky, his eyes narrowing. "He's here?"

"Yeah, he's in Fairy Falls." I tried to peer past him into the hallway. How much of what I saw was an illusion and how much was real? It was impossible to tell, but the glamour pouring out of every facet of the cottage was unmistakeable.

"So they've come back," he said. "To take the town for their own."

"Some fairies would support them," I replied. "Since the witches drove the fairies out of town, some of the fairies believe the hunters are the only people who might help them get back what they lost. They don't know that the hunters' leader *is* a fairy."

I tried to watch his face as I spoke, but the glowing illusion of the house kept drawing my eye. Then a glint caught my eye from behind the window and my gaze landed on a spherical object as black as pitch, a stark contrast to the shimmering lights of the glamour that made up this place.

The Seeing Stone was *here*, in Conor's house. He'd taken it for himself. Had Conor been the one who'd given my dad up to the hunters? Was that how he'd got his hands on it?

As I made an imperceptible movement towards the house, the fairy barred my path. As he did so, the glamour of the house wavered behind him. Underneath the gleaming illusion, it was probably a run-down cottage like the one my mother had lived in. He'd covered it with an illusion and yanked it out of the everyday world using his magic, which made it the perfect place to hide a stolen Seeing Stone where even the witches and the hunters wouldn't be able to find it.

I should have known finding another fairy would be too good to be true.

"That Seeing Stone." I pointed over his shoulder. "It doesn't belong to you."

His jaw twitched. "Blair, if I were you, I'd leave."

"I don't think so," I said. "I'm going to talk to my dad at nine tomorrow. If I asked him where the Seeing Stone was hidden, would he know you were the one who had it?"

His eyes narrowed. "You can't out-magic me, Blair. You're too human."

"The Seeing Stone belongs to the regional witch council," I told him. "I know what the witches did to the fairies, Conor, but the hunters will make life even worse for us if I don't give the Seeing Stone back to them. And my dad will never walk free again."

"You have no idea what the witches did to us," he said. "*Your* ancestors, Blair. Did you think you could get away with hiding the truth from me?"

"I might have told you if you hadn't unleashed a storm on my head for even mentioning them." This was all going wrong. "Let me guess—you hate my dad for choosing to be with Tanith, too. And you hate the witches for driving you out of town, so you want the hunters to take their place."

"The witches banished us from the world," he said. "They're a blight on the town and deserve to fall."

"Excuse me? The fairies got my father arrested. My mother *died* because of what they did." My voice cracked. "You don't see me blaming every single one of you for that, do you?"

Outrage crossed his face. Above our heads, thunder crackled, and the sky split with lightning. At the same time, the garden *moved,* the plants rearing up like monstrous creatures. Conor himself glowed with eerie light which made him look positively demonic.

But I had a scary monster on my side, too. Sky reared up behind me, his monstrous form dominating the garden. Meanwhile I snapped my fingers and took flight, hovering out of range of the plants and looking down on the house. There was only one door, so I'd have to fly past him to get my hands on the Seeing Stone.

The instant I descended, Conor barred my way. "I will not allow you take what belongs to the fairies alone, Blair."

I flew above him, my wings beating. "That Seeing Stone is not yours. You shouldn't have it."

"Neither should the witches," he said.

"The hunters are worse than any of the witch covens," I insisted. "Look what they did to my dad, even though he was a fairy himself. If I don't get that Seeing Stone to the Inquisitor, he'll drive *you* out of town next as soon as he learns you exist."

"You're lying." Another wave of lightning split the sky and a torrent of rain drenched me. Sky yowled as he continued to bat away at the plants with his giant paws.

"Listen to me," I said, raising my voice over the clamour of the storm. "The Inquisitor *is* a fairy, and I bet he can see and hear your magic right now. You're pretty much waving a blazing light in the air and telling him to come and find you. Even if I don't give him the Seeing Stone, he'll find it himself. I can guarantee it. He wants Fairy Falls under his command and he'll gladly trample everyone else in his path to get his way."

"You're lying," he said. "You want the Seeing Stone for yourself, don't you? You haven't even told me who this Inquisitor is."

"He's…" Inspiration struck. I reached into my pocket,

whipped out the photo of the Inquisitor and shoved it at him. "That's him. This picture was taken decades ago, and he doesn't look any different today. I've never seen him without his glamour on."

He stared at the photograph, the rain fading out as his gaze fixed on the man in the centre. "That's Rowe Clearwater, the Prince of the Clearwater Court. Even with that disguise on, I recognise his face."

"That's his real name?" He was a prince, too? "He's the leader of the paranormal hunters, and he's here in Fairy Falls. He also probably saw that display of your magic."

He waved a hand and the plants stopped moving, while the last of the rain petered out. Sky shook rainwater out of his fur and hissed his displeasure as he shrank back to normal cat-size again.

"Rowe Clearwater is the leader of the paranormal hunters?" Conor said. "How is that possible?"

"How long have you been hiding?" I queried. "The Inquisitor was the one who sent the hunters after my dad when he came to you for help. Did you give him up to the hunters? Tell me the truth."

"There was nothing I could have done to prevent them from finding him." In the background, silence filled the garden once again. "Your father grew restless and chose to leave the safety of this glamoured haven. Before he left, he told me to watch the Seeing Stone and not to give it to another soul. He didn't mention that he had a child."

"I was in the normal world at the time," I said. "But I need that Seeing Stone. If I don't give it to the Inquisitor, my dad will remain in jail for the rest of his life, and I'll have to leave Fairy Falls. The hunters will step in to take control of the town, and believe me, they're worse than the witches could ever be. They'll find your hiding place. I can guarantee they will."

He was silent for a moment. "If Rowe Clearwater wants the Seeing Stone, then it can only be for his own gain. The Stone would grant him total control over any fairy who stands before him."

"Any… fairy?" My heart stuttered. "I thought it was used to see the future."

"That's just one of the Seeing Stone's uses," he said. "If Rowe Clearwater gets his hands on it, he will use it to consolidate his own power over paranormals and non-paranormals alike, and the witches will stand by and let him do it."

So that was his aim? "Do the witches know what the Seeing Stone can do?"

I found it hard to believe they didn't, and yet nobody had mentioned its side effect of being able to exert control over anyone it was used on. No wonder the council had been willing to condemn my dad for refusing to tell them where he'd hidden it.

"Not all of them," he said, his eyes flaring with anger. "However, I imagine Rowe Clearwater has allies among them."

Yes. He must, if he was confident that they'd let him keep the stone for himself. Then no fairy or human would have the strength to stand up to him.

"Not all the witches," I said. "The new Head Witch is one of my closest friends, and the coven leader, Madame Grey… she's a good person, too. The majority of the witches want to keep the hunters out of town, and they won't let the Inquisitor take the Seeing Stone. I can promise that."

I hope.

"You had better not be lying," he said. "Do you have the Pixie-Glass?"

"Not yet, but it'll be here soon," I evaded, not entirely trusting his word. "I have until tomorrow to use it to contact the fairies before I have to show my face to the Inquisitor."

"In that case, I will give you this." He walked into the house and through a door on the right-hand side. A minute later, he emerged, wings beating behind him, and he handed me the Seeing Stone. "Do not let Clearwater use this."

"I won't." I closed my hand around the dark sphere, marvelling at how light it felt. "I'm going to see Madame Grey and explain exactly what it's capable of. She won't let the Inquisitor get his hands on it. She's already been contacting all her potential allies from the regional witch council, so we can root out which ones are supporting the Inquisitor. If you like, you can talk to them yourself and tell them who the Inquisitor really is. I'm sure they'd be grateful for your input."

I had my doubts he'd be willing to leave his bubble, but the weight of the sphere in my hand bolstered me.

"Then I will wait to hear from you, Blair," he said. "Thank you."

"I'll try not to screw this up."

Putting the Seeing Stone in my pocket, I left the garden and joined Sky on the path. As I stepped out of the illusion, a flurry of movement rustled the treetops, and through a gap in the canopy, I glimpsed dozens of broomsticks soaring through the sky. *What's going on this time?*

I quickened my pace and flew through the forest,

halting when the gaps in the trees grew large enough to show a number of witches and wizards had gathered on the lakeshore. Sky gave a soft *miaow,* his fur standing on end.

Had the Inquisitor already called all the regional coven representatives to town in order to witness me hand over the Seeing Stone? I didn't see him among their group, but I needed to tell Madame Grey they were here. If she didn't already know. Maybe *she'd* invited them... but I couldn't count on it.

It was almost fully dark by now, and Sky was a blur at my side as I flew towards home and transformed back into my human form to let myself into the house. Sky padded in after me, entering the living room.

Alissa's brows shot into the air. "What happened to you? Your hair looks like you've been flying in a storm and you're all wet."

Did I really look that bad? "Conor Underwood and I had a misunderstanding. Also, you should know, there's about a dozen witches gathering near the lake right this moment. Please tell me Madame Grey's the one who called them here."

"My grandmother mentioned calling the regional witch council here for a meeting," she said. "A last-minute one."

"While the Inquisitor is still here?" I said, confused. "Is he that confident I'll get the Seeing Stone back? Wait, how much does Madame Grey actually know about his ultimatum?"

"As much as I could tell her over the phone," said Alissa. "She talked to Veronica, too, and I got the impression both of them were calling all the members of the regional witch council they had on their contacts list."

"She must have figured that waiting until next week's meeting would be leaving it too late," I surmised. "Maybe she thinks I can figure out which of them is supporting the hunters, but she's putting an awful lot of faith in me."

Alissa blinked. "Come again?"

"At least one of the council members is on the Inquisitor's side," I explained. "If they weren't, then my dad would have given the Seeing Stone back to them without expecting it to end up in the Inquisitor's hands. Conor just told me that the Inquisitor can use its power to control anyone. I think he wants it to ensure no fairy ever challenges him again, and I also think he has a plan to make the witches let him take it."

Her eyes widened. "Hang on, did you say you know where it is? The Seeing Stone?"

"You might say that." I pulled it out of my pocket. "Conor Underwood has been hiding it in his house since my dad left and got arrested. Hence our misunderstanding. Anyway, he has a few things he wants to say to the hunters as well."

"You *have* it?" she said. "Why not give it to witches yourself?"

"Only when I'm sure they won't hand it to the Inquisitor," I said. "Can you imagine him having even more power than he already does? I think my dad knew he wanted it for himself and that's why he took it. I'd say that's a good reason for risking his freedom to keep it hidden."

"I suppose—" Her phone rang. "I'll get that."

While she answered the call, I carried the Seeing Stone

into my bedroom, pursued by Sky. Then I sat down on the bed and examined the glass ball…

…and saw my own face staring back. The flat black surface reflected my room back at me, and unlike a regular crystal ball, it didn't block my magic.

But could the Seeing Stone show me a way to win? I was out of any better ideas, so I gazed into its depths.

The surface turned transparent, and I tumbled head-first into an illusion.

I was flying. The ground soaring away beneath me. At my side, someone else flew. A man, who looked just like me. Curly dark hair, pale skin, dark eyes… and wings.

Dad.

Was I seeing the past? The future?

The wind picked up behind me, and I looked over my shoulder. Panic suffused my dad's expression. "They're here, Blair."

Together, we landed, and found ourselves surrounded by hunters, all of whom pointed their weapons at us. At the head of them stood the Inquisitor, a black gleaming crystal ball in his hand.

My dad shouted my name, but the hunters were already dragging me away. The Inquisitor smiled as my dad and I were wrenched apart.

The illusion let me go, and I gasped, staggering against my bed and gripping the ball in one hand. Had I seen a vision of what my dad had seen in the glass himself? If he'd seen the hunters split us apart, he might have assumed that that would be my fate if I ever set foot in the paranormal world… and if the Inquisitor ever got his hands on the Seeing Stone.

Sadness gripped me. My dad had wanted to protect me from the fate he'd seen, and he'd gone as far as to let himself get arrested and imprisoned. He'd even hidden the Seeing Stone with someone he trusted so its power couldn't be used to control the other fairies—and if I let the Inquisitor have it, his sacrifice would have all been for nothing.

The doorbell rang, making me jump. *Please tell me the Inquisitor isn't here.* I leapt off the bed and put the Seeing Stone into my pocket again, while Sky nudged the bedroom door open.

"Blair, Nathan's here," Alissa said.

"He has the Pixie-Glass." I walked back to the living room, pulling the black and white photo out of my pocket. "Nathan's dad told me. He also gave me this."

"Nathan's dad?" said Alissa. Then she saw the photo in my hand. "Is that the Inquisitor?"

"Yeah, it's proof that he's older than he seems," I said. "Conor Underwood can back me up, but I'm not sure this'll be enough proof for the council. I was supposed to take the Pixie-Glass to Conor and get him to call his other fairy allies to back me up, but now the regional witch council is already here, I don't know if we'll have the time."

The doorbell rang again. I ran to answer it, and found Nathan stood on the doorstep, holding the Pixie-Glass in both hands.

"Did your dad tell you—"

"He did." He eyed the ball-shaped lump in my pocket. "Did you find the Seeing Stone?"

"Yeah," I said. "Turns out it was hidden for a good reason. Can you keep hold of the glass?"

"I thought you needed it now."

"I need to see the regional witch council first, and they're already here," I said. "I also need backup."

"You want to talk to the witches now?" he said. "Wasn't it Madame Grey who called them?"

"Apparently, but at least one of them is on the Inquisitor's side," I said. "For all we know, they brought reinforcements, too."

His eyes widened. "Would you be able to figure out which of them is supporting the hunters if you spoke to them?"

"Possibly, but I need backup," I said. "On account of the fact that the Inquisitor is prepared to use my dad's case as proof that I'm an untrustworthy liar."

"Samuel is on his way," Alissa told me. "I can ask him to meet you at the witches' place. I'll be right behind you. He can read the minds of every one of the witches and expose the traitor."

"Assuming he's allowed into the meeting," I added. "I can't let the Inquisitor get to them first, but he must know they're here."

"What do you want to do with the Seeing Stone?" asked Alissa.

"I can't leave it unattended," I said. "I think the best thing I can do is take it with me. Better than risking it ending up in the wrong hands. If this goes well, I can hand it back to the witches there and then. If not, the Inquisitor will take it for his own whether I have it with me or not."

I didn't add, *then it'll all be over.* Judging by their grave expressions, the others had heard my unsaid words all the same.

"Then I'll walk you there." Nathan took my arm. "If I'm allowed into the meeting, I'll be right beside you."

"Look after the Pixie-Glass," I told him. "I don't know if my dad is on the other side. If I knew for sure, I'd use it to speak to him, but I'm not giving Mrs Dailey the chance to gloat at me again."

"Yeah, better not risk it," said Alissa, and gave me a quick hug. "I'll be behind you. Sky, too. Right?"

"Miaow," said Sky, who presumably knew he wouldn't be allowed into the meeting. The Inquisitor could see through glamour, after all.

But this was my last chance.

Nathan and I left the house and headed towards the witches' headquarters. It was time for a final reckoning with the Inquisitor.

15

After parting ways with Nathan and Alissa, I walked the rest of the way to the witches' head-quarters alone. The lobby was empty, and when I entered the meeting room, a single person waited inside.

The Inquisitor. A bolt of fear hit me, and he arched a brow at the sight of me.

"You're here sooner than I expected, Blair," he said. "Did my assistant take pity on you and hand over the Pixie-Glass?"

Anger stifled my fear. "Maybe your fellow hunters aren't as loyal as you think."

"How interesting." He gestured to the seat at his side. "Do come in. I'm expecting company, but I believe Madame Grey has gone to greet her new visitors before she brings them to meet me."

I didn't move. "Since when was there going to be a council meeting tonight? I thought it was supposed to be next week."

I'd also thought the Inquisitor was sending Nathan's

brother in his place. What was Madame Grey thinking by inviting them here?

"I cannot pretend to know why Madame Grey chose to invite them here tonight, but the Seeing Stone belonged to the regional witch council before your father stole it," he said. "I think they'll be grateful to know you intend to return it to their hands."

Right. "I thought I had until tomorrow morning to find and return the stone. Besides, if you're so confident I can find it, then why did you wait until now to ask me to retrieve the stone? It's been months since our last meeting, yet you've known all along that my dad was the one who took it."

"Well, for one thing, I didn't know if you could be trusted to do the right thing," he said. "Your mother's rebellious nature sprang to mind when I first heard of your exploits here in the magical world. I believed you had the potential to be of use to us, certainly, but if you'd learned your father had stolen something of such value, you might have taken it for yourself."

"My dad didn't steal the stone because he wanted it for himself." My voice rose. "As for my mum, she died to protect me from the hunters. Am I expected to forget you're the reason she's dead?"

"Certainly not," he said. "Your mother wasn't supposed to die. Her fate was a tragedy."

Anger I'd never felt before hit me like a train, rendering me unable to speak for a moment. "It was *murder.*"

Several sparks shot from my hands. He rose fluidly from his seat, all traces of false congeniality erased from his expression. "I'll kindly ask you to keep your magic under control, Blair. Your mother was not murdered. A team of hunters was sent to look for Braden Eventide, but Tanith refused to reveal his whereabouts. She then fought back and died in the attempt."

"Yet you still expect me to work for you?" My voice cracked, but I held his gaze. He truly was monstrous.

"You're still under the delusion that you have a choice, Blair?" He shook his head. "As I said—once your father was in captivity, our disagreement was over. And when we have the Seeing Stone, we will be able to mend things between us, too, Blair."

The weight of the Seeing Stone in my pocket seemed to increase with every word he spoke. At least he couldn't read my thoughts, but I was in way over my head. Worse, the sound of voices and footsteps came from outside the room.

"The council is here," he added. "Let us greet them."

Madame Grey entered the room, followed by several more witches. Some I knew, some I didn't. Rebecca accompanied them, carrying the sceptre. *Dammit, I wanted her to stay out of this.* But it seemed the scheduled meeting would take place here and now, and Madame Grey had seen to it herself. I really hoped she had a better plan than I did, because mine had already collapsed around my ears.

Behind the witches came the hunters, who rallied around the Inquisitor. Their plain clothing contrasted the brightness of the witches' hats and cloaks, while their expressions radiated hostility. Especially when Nathan walked in, along with Erin and Buck. The ex-hunters pointedly positioned themselves on the same side of the room as the witches, while several others entered to join them. Chief Donovan of the pack, Vincent the Vampire, and even the Elf King, surrounded by a contingent of guards. I found myself a seat, acutely aware of the number of eyes on me. I'd little expected to end up stuck in a meeting room surrounded by both allies and enemies, with the fate of the whole town resting in the balance.

Rebecca met my gaze and gave a brave nod, clutching the sceptre in one hand. Madame Grey nodded to me, too, indicating the visiting witches with a subtle gesture. She wanted me to look at them? I couldn't read minds, like Samuel and Vincent, but this group of witches were the true owners of the Seeing Stone.

Or were they? Conor Underwood had said it had originally belonged to the fairies, but he wasn't here. I'd lost my chance to get more of the fairies on my side, so I'd have to root out the Inquisitor's supporters on my own.

As the meeting began with introductions, I scanned the newcomers, trying to memorise their names. Clove Darwood, their leader, sat closest to the Inquisitor. Her dark hair was twisted into an elaborate topknot, as though she'd quickly styled it before leaving for the last-minute meeting. Despite her stern expression, I didn't detect any suspicious vibes from her. No glamour, anyway. My gaze slid onto the others, though a voice in the back of my head whispered that I shouldn't have expected it to be easy to pinpoint the Inquisitor's supporters from first impressions. It wasn't like they'd have a sign hanging over their head, was it?

A glimmer in the corner of my eye drew my attention to a blond witch sitting in the centre of the row. Her appearance was unremarkable... except for that odd glimmering light. *Is she wearing an illusion spell?*

During a lull in the introductions, I rose to my feet, pointing at her. "What spell are you wearing?"

"Spell?" she said. "You're Blair Wilkes, aren't you? The fairy-witch."

Whispers broke out among the new arrivals. My face heated, but I remained standing. "And you are?"

"Me?" she said. "Brigit Claire, a representative of the regional witch council of the northwest."

"I assume that since I can't see through the illusion you're wearing, you have something to hide," I added. "Since it's hidden by a fairy glamour."

"Why, the cheek of it—"

"Let her have her moment," said the Inquisitor, sounding amused. "Blair, what is your problem?"

A fresh wave of anger washed over me at his mocking tone. "I have the ability to see through any illusion, even fairy glamours. That's my witch talent."

As my gaze went back to the indignant witch, the gleaming light resolved into the shape of a pendant hanging around her neck.

"She speaks true," Vincent said from across the table. "I also cannot read her thoughts, so I assume whatever she's wearing prevents her mind from being read."

Brigit shifted in her seat. "I'll kindly ask you to stop these accusations. We have come here because Madame Grey claims to have the location of an item which has been missing from our property for quite some time."

"Not missing, but stolen," added the Inquisitor. "By none other than Blair's father."

All eyes turned to me. It seemed the Inquisitor had abandoned his old plan in favour of publicly humiliating me and forcing me to admit my dad was a thief in front of the entire council. Which meant I could say goodbye to any chance of winning their support.

I remained on my feet, trying to keep my panic from showing on my face. "Were you aware of what the Seeing Stone is capable of? Or did the Inquisitor keep that piece of information to himself?"

"You admit your father is a thief?" said Brigit Claire.

"The Seeing Stone was stolen four years ago or more," Madame Grey interjected. "I have read a copy of the reports myself, and three witches in this room were present at the trial, including you, Brigit. I'm intrigued to know why the reports were kept secret from the other members of the council."

So she did do the research. A wave of gratitude bolstered me and prevented me from sinking back into my seat in a fit of embarrassment.

"We left the final verdict to the hunters," said Brigit, her face flushing. "We trusted that they would eventually gain the information they needed from their prisoner."

"You thought wrong," I said, speaking over the murmur of voices. "My dad hid the Seeing Stone because he believed the Inquisitor planned to use it for his own gain. He was willing to risk his freedom to keep it safe—"

"Enough." The Inquisitor snapped his fingers, and silence descended. At once, I couldn't move an inch, and from the alarm rippling through the others, the spell had affected them, too.

The Inquisitor was even more powerful than I'd feared. He hadn't even needed the Seeing Stone's magic to bring us all under his control. Sweat beaded on my forehead as I fought to move, but my body remained locked to my seat.

In one smooth motion, the Inquisitor rose to his feet. He strode the length of the table, past the council members who sat frozen in their seats, until he stopped right behind me. All the hairs on my arms stood on end as he reached out and took the Seeing Stone from my pocket.

No.

Gasps rose from the assembled paranormals and hunters as the spell momentarily broke. The Inquisitor raised the Seeing Stone into the air, and the entire meeting room stilled once again. The witches' expressions turned glazed, and at first, I feared the Seeing Stone already held them in the grip of its power.

Then Clove Darwood spoke. "So it's true."

"Blair found the Seeing Stone where her father hid it, before his arrest," said the Inquisitor. "It's been missing for all this time. I trust she has a good reason for keeping it hidden inside her pocket during this meeting."

"I didn't—" I tried to say, but my body remained immobile and my mouth was locked shut. The others didn't even seem to notice. Maybe they assumed guilt had rendered me mute. Panicking, I tried to meet someone's gaze, anyone's, but none came to my rescue.

He'd taken the Seeing Stone. If he left here with it in his hands... I didn't like to imagine the consequences.

As the Inquisitor strode away from my chair, something furred brushed my ankle. I spotted Sky's mismatched eyes blinking up at me from underneath the table. He must have sneaked into the meeting after all. I worried briefly about him being spotted, but everyone's eyes were on the Seeing Stone... at least until Sky leapt up and batted it out of the Inquisitor's hands.

For an instant, his expression froze, while the stone hit the table with a jarring thud that shattered the silence. The Seeing Stone rolled to a halt on the table, and mutters broke out among the others at the same time as my body unfroze. Relief washed over me, and I let Sky climb into my arms.

"That," said the Inquisitor, "is a fairy cat. You brought him here to help you steal back the Seeing Stone, didn't you?"

"Sky doesn't do anything he doesn't want to." With my body unfrozen, my fear devolved to simple nerves and I babbled. "You can't expect a cat to ignore a shiny ball, can you? Besides, the Seeing Stone belonged to the fairies before the witches, which I think is pretty relevant at the moment."

"Whoever it belonged to before the witches is of no consequence," said the Inquisitor. "Your father stole it and lied about its location—"

"Let her speak," interjected Madame Grey. "I for one would like to hear what Blair has to say about the fairies' relationship to the Seeing Stone."

I kept an eye on the Seeing Stone, ignoring the Inquisitor's angry stare, and addressed the room. "I don't know how much you all know about how Fairy Falls originated, but it was founded by a group of roaming fairies. They lived behind the waterfall at first. Then another fairy, called Rowe Clearwater, came to the area."

"We've heard enough," said Brigit, reaching for the stone. "This is ours."

Sky turned into his giant self and jumped onto the table. While everyone gaped at him, Sky positioned himself defensively in front of the Seeing Stone, and I spoke into the shocked silence.

"Rowe Clearwater believed all fairies who didn't belong to his Court were a nuisance and were to be driven out," I said. "So he made a deal with the witches whose coven ruled the town, and they worked together to drive the other fairies away. Since then, they've remained exiled, and many of the fairies blamed the witches for their fate."

"Is that true?" asked Clove Darwood, addressing Madame Grey.

"To my knowledge, it is," said Madame Grey. "Go on, Blair."

"That all changed when one of the descendants of the original coven, Tanith Wildflower, fell in love with a fairy," I went on. "Braden Eventide was his name, and he was a Prince of the Court of Eventide. Their relationship caused much strife among the exiles, as many of the fairies believed him to have betrayed them by loving my mother at all. Meanwhile, many of the witches believed Tanith to have betrayed *them*. When Rowe Clearwater found out, he sent his allies after both of them in an attempt to destroy them."

My heart beat faster when it hit me that everyone was watching me now—and that they were listening to every word.

"Tanith and Braden had a child," I continued. "Since they were still on the run, they left her in the normal world to keep her safe from Rowe Clearwater and his allies. Eventually, however, Tanith was caught and died defending her own life. Braden remained in hiding until he found out his child might be in danger despite all he'd done to keep her safe."

"You're the child," said Clove Darwood. "But your father stole the Seeing Stone, did he not?"

"I haven't spoken to him face to face in my entire life, so I can't give his side of the story," I said. "From what I gather, he wanted to ensure my safety, and he took the stone and used its power to see into my future. The stone's vision showed him that if he brought me into the paranormal world, we would both suffer."

A ripple of noise spread among the witches.

"If that's the case, then why did he not return the stone once he had the knowledge he wanted?" Clove queried.

"Because that's not all the stone can be used for," I said. "It also has the capacity to boost any fairy's magical talent and can even be used to enable them to exert control over anyone they desire. Like any magical artefact, it's dangerous in the wrong hands."

"Really?" said the woman on Clove's right-hand-side. "I never heard of such a thing."

The Inquisitor spoke up. "I know you've suffered some personal tragedies, Blair, but there's no need to concoct lies—"

"Plainly," Nathan said loudly, "the only way to confirm Blair's father's story is to speak to the man himself."

All the air seemed to leave the room as he held up the Pixie-Glass and placed it on the table.

"What's that?" said Clove Darwood.

"The Inquisitor gave this Pixie-Glass to my brother," Nathan said. "And he generously loaned it to us so we could contact Braden Eventide himself."

My dad's face appeared in the glass. The breath

punched out of my lungs. Even if I hadn't seen him in the vision the Seeing Stone had shown me, I would still have known he was my dad. He looked just like I did when I wore my fairy form. Wings extended behind his shoulders, and his pointed ears parted his long hair.

"Every word Blair said is true," said my father. "I stole the Seeing Stone in order to protect my child, and to protect the magical world from Rowe Clearwater's ambition to use the stone for his own ends. Blair—show them what he really is."

His words sent a bolt of purpose through me. I reached out and snatched the Seeing Stone from the table. At once, a rush of power rose within me.

The Inquisitor moved towards me, but I snapped my fingers, grabbing the threads of the glamour swirling around him—glamour which shone bright as day.

Wings appeared behind his shoulders, brightening the room. A chorus of gasps rose from among the gathering witches, several of whom leapt to their feet.

"Traitor!" shouted the Elf King.

"Traitor!" Chief Donovan shouted a heartbeat later, and then looked startled to hear his exclamation echoed by the elves with twice the enthusiasm.

The Inquisitor glanced around, a flicker of panic appearing on his face. "How dare you disrespect me?"

"You aren't who you're pretending to be," said one of the witches. "Are you?"

"Inquisitor Hare's real name is Rowe Clearwater, the other fairy from the story I just told you," I told the gathering crowd. "My father knew he planned to use the Seeing Stone to consolidate his power, but since the hunters imprisoned my dad before he could warn anyone, he had no choice but to keep silent through their attempts to interrogate him."

"Correct," added my dad from the glass. "Now the Inquisitor leads the paranormal hunters, but he has always feared the other fairies would rise to displace him, haven't you, Rowe?"

The Inquisitor paled. His eyes looked freakishly large in his fairy form, and despite the sheer overwhelming force of the power radiating from him, he still seemed less intimidating. Or maybe it was the equally potent power humming from the shining black glass ball I held in my hands, and the fact that the Inquisitor could no longer hide his true nature.

"I've heard enough from you, Eventide," the Inquisitor said to my father. "Now, Blair, give the Seeing Stone back to the witches at once."

"And what of you?" asked one of the witches. "Are you really a fairy?"

"Looks that way to me," another commented. "Have you been lying to us all along?"

Questions rose from among the assembled crowd, and the Inquisitor had no answers to give. Nor did his remaining allies, come to that. The other hunters stared at their boss, stunned into silence by the wings extending behind his shoulders and his strange alien-like appearance.

"I have another issue to raise," Nathan said. "When I obtained this Pixie-Glass, I asked for a local fairy's help so I could use it. Imagine my surprise when I found a known criminal sitting on the other side of the glass. Mrs Dailey is supposed to be in isolation, is she not?"

"Mrs Dailey?" said one of the witches. "Isn't she the

one who tried to take over Fairy Falls's coven and manipulated her youngest daughter?"

"The very same," said Madame Grey.

A fresh ripple of mutters travelled among the witches.

"She worked with the hunters."

"Has he been granting her freedoms when she's supposed to be under tight security?"

"Enough!" shouted the Inquisitor. "I am the leader of the hunters in this region and I will not tolerate this level of insubordination—"

"You're head of nothing," said Clove Darwood. "We're the leading authority. The hunters aren't. And besides, you don't look anything like a hunter to me. The question remains… who among my fellow witches assisted you in hiding the details of the theft of the Seeing Stone?"

At that, Brigit Claire tried to run, but Vincent got there first, barring her path. Several other witches moved in to restrain her, deaf to her protests.

The Inquisitor turned to me, a wild look in his eye. "What do you want from me?"

"I want my dad to be set free." I held up the Seeing Stone. "And you to swear not to use this Seeing Stone again. It might belong to the fairies, but you have no right to claim domination over anyone else."

"He will be set free," he ground out. "But *that* does not belong to you—"

"I'll give it up to the council," I said. "The council, *not* your personal allies. After that, I just want to see my dad."

"Well, of course," said Clove Darwood, reaching out a hand.

Warily, I passed her the Seeing Stone. Vincent caught my eye and winked, while Sky bounded into my arms. As the witches took the stone, I sat down, dizzy with relief. My dad was going to be set free, and the Inquisitor stood stock-still for an instant, as though his defeat had rendered him inert. Meanwhile, Nathan laid the Pixie-Glass down on the table in front of me.

My dad leaned closer to the glass to speak to me. "Blair, my case will take some time to review, but I'll come straight to you as soon as it's done. I promise."

My eyes burned with tears. "Of course."

"Hey!" someone shouted. "Where'd he go?"

My head snapped up, automatically glancing at the Inquisitor… but he was no longer there. "Did he glamour himself invisible?"

I snapped my fingers, but he didn't reappear. Even when the witches converged on the spot where he'd been standing with the Seeing Stone in hand, there were no signs of him inside the room. *I should have known he'd have one last trick up his sleeve.*

Yet the day had ended in triumph. My dad would soon walk free, and he was coming home to Fairy Falls.

16

The weekend couldn't come soon enough.

As my dad had guessed, it'd taken a long while for the paperwork for his release to be approved. I'd been told he'd be out by the end of the weekend, but to say I had no focus at work for the rest of the week was an understatement. Luckily my boss was understanding. So were my co-workers, come to that.

"Anything you need, Blair?" Rob asked. "More coffee?"

"If I have any more coffee, I'll be on floating on the ceiling without even needing to have my wings out," I replied.

Lizzie grinned at me across the desk. "I can take the blame for that one. I thought it would help your focus, but maybe not."

"We love you anyway," added Bethan.

The printer chirped an agreement. It had been singing *We are the Champions* at random intervals all week, courtesy of a quick adjustment from Lizzie.

"I think the boss has been holding back our more difficult clients, though," said Lizzie. "That, or enough hunters have quit that that all our regular clients have been hiring ex-hunters instead."

"I don't think that many people left the hunters," said Rob. "Not that I've heard."

"I heard they're pretty much lost without their leader, though," Bethan said, with a significant look at me. "Nobody's seen him since he pulled that disappearing act."

"Believe me, I wish I knew where he ran off to," I said. "Maybe he went back to fairyland."

I wouldn't lie, his absence worried me a little, but at least Mrs Dailey's privileges had been taken away, and she wouldn't be coming out of the LPFP anytime soon. I no longer had to fear her watching over my shoulder.

"I wouldn't complain about the lack of clients," added Lizzie. "It sounds like everyone has a lot going on, what with the regional witch council losing a few of its members as well as the hunters."

"Yeah, they do." The door creaked open behind me, and I turned around as my boss walked into the office.

"Blair?" said Veronica. "Come with me."

My heart jumped. I hadn't had a full conversation with her since I'd broken down in her office the other day. I didn't expect her to punish me or anything, but I still wasn't quite sure what to expect from our first real conversation since my dad had been granted his freedom.

I rose to my feet and walked with her to her office, which had the same setup as last time. The bright flowers and tree stumps still reminded me of the glamoured bubble in which Conor lived.

"Madame Grey wants to see you," Veronica told me. "I

think it's about your father. You can leave work early if you like."

"He's free?" My heart leapt again, this time for an entirely different reason. "I—thanks so much. Thank you."

I backed out of her office, flashed a smile at a startled Callie, and ran to grab my bag from the office. One garbled goodbye later, I left via the automatic doors. I practically flew down the road to the witches' headquarters, at which point I slowed down. Trying to rein in my excitement, I reached Madame Grey's office and knocked.

"Come in," she called.

I walked into the office. My dad was nowhere to be seen, but Madame Grey's wide smile greeted me.

"I heard from the LPFP that your father left their facility today," she said. "He should be on his way here right now."

Tears leapt to my eyes. "He's coming to Fairy Falls?"

"According to the call I just got," she said. "He'll be here within the hour, I expect. If he flies."

"I think he will." I swallowed back my tears. "I never thanked you for backing me up against the Inquisitor. I'm sorry it almost went so badly wrong."

"You did fine, Blair," she said. "Better than fine. We have nothing to fear from the Inquisitor any longer."

"But—he got away," I said. "You don't think he'll come back?"

"I think we'll be more than ready if he does," she said. "I've also put out word that we'll welcome any fairies who want to move back to Fairy Falls. That friend of yours, Conor Underwood, is helping us."

"That's great," I said. "Thank you. For everything."

I left her office and nearly walked into Blythe of all

people. Catching my balance, I saw Rebecca standing behind her, holding the sceptre.

"What's up with you?" Blythe said. "You look like you're about to cry."

"Nothing bad," I said. "Why are you here?"

"To see Madame Grey," she said. "The newly reformed regional witch council is holding a meeting to talk about the Seeing Stone and the future of the hunters, and I'm going with Rebecca to meet them."

"Oh, good." I'd expected to have to accompany her myself, but I was only one person with a lot of demands on my time and it was nice to have someone else take the reins for a bit. "I hope it goes well."

"Why aren't you at work?" asked Rebecca, as observant as ever.

"My dad's coming here," I said. "They just let him out of jail, so I have to go and meet him."

"He is?" said Blythe. "Um. Good. I'm glad."

"Sure. Uh. See you later." I turned away before things could get any more awkward. The two of us would probably never be friendly with one another, but it was nice to have her support, however strange it might seem.

"Good luck, Blair," Rebecca called after me as I left.

I headed to the hospital first, where Alissa was working. There, I found old Ava wandering around the waiting room, her wand sticking out from behind her ear and a happy look on her face.

"There you are, Briar," she said cheerily. "It's a lovely day."

"Are you supposed to be out of your room?" I asked.

"No," said an exasperated Alissa, emerging through a

nearby door. "What're you doing here, Blair? Something wrong?"

"My dad's free," I said. "He's on his way here. Soon. If I'm late home, that's where I am."

"That's wonderful news!" She strode over and hugged me. "Let me know how it goes, okay?"

"Will do." I released her and smiled at Ava. "Thanks for the warning, and for trying to help."

"The winged one is no threat to you any longer, Blair," she said. "You made Tanith proud."

Alissa looked perplexed. "Um…"

"Long story." I backed towards the door. "I'll tell you later."

While Alissa coaxed Ava back to the ward, I left the hospital and flew back to our house. I was pretty sure Sky would be quick to figure out my dad was back in town, but I wanted to ask him to come with me in case he hadn't heard the news.

I opened the door and peered into the flat. Roald lay on the sofa, but not Sky. Had he gone to the bookshop? He might be with Vincent again. After checking the whole flat, I left and headed back to the high street.

From there, I made my way to the bookshop. I pushed open the door and found Vincent the vampire in conversation with Chief Donovan of the pack. As I stared at the pair of them in bewilderment, Sky peered out from behind the vampire's legs and came over to me.

"Sky." I scratched him behind the ears. "What're you doing here? Did you hear my dad's coming back to town?"

"I believe he did," said Vincent, pausing in his conversation with the chief of the werewolf pack. "I also believe he's on his way to the lake right now."

I frowned. "You can hear his thoughts from this far off?"

"Not his," he said. "Your little friend there has stayed in touch with several other fairy cats in the area."

"Sky, you never told me you were still in touch with the others,' I said.

"Miaow."

Chief Donovan looked between us. "What on earth are you talking about?"

"My dad is coming to town," I explained. "He's a fairy. Do tell your pack to leave him alone, won't you?"

"I assume your father knows better than to trespass on our territory."

"He's been here before, don't worry." I looked down at Sky. "Want to meet my dad in person?"

"Miaow," he said.

We left the bookshop and walked down the high street together until we reached the route leading to the lake. When the sound of the crashing waterfall grew louder, I brought out my fairy wings and flew up the path alongside the forest.

Then I halted, seeing a distant figure approaching the town and growing closer by the second. My dad must be wearing his human glamour, since I saw no wings as he walked towards me. He must have flown to get here this quickly, though.

I forced myself to keep moving, worry spiking inside me. What if he wasn't as pleased to see me as I'd expected? He might have given up his freedom for my sake, but I'd screwed up at least half the opportunities I'd been given. Besides, he might not like me when he got to know me better, since we hadn't met in person at all. A quick conversation via the Pixie-Glass didn't count.

He quickened his pace, seeing me, and we met halfway across the path in front of the lake. Then without a word, he wrapped me in a hug. I hugged him back, my worries melting away.

"Miaow." Sky shoved his way between us, demanding a stroke.

"Oh." Dad looked startled at the sight of the little cat wrapping around his ankles. "Is that a fairy cat?"

"This is Sky," I said. "Sky, meet my dad. Sky is my familiar. Kind of. Not in the usual sense, though. He's more of a friend."

"Yes, fairy cats can be quite independent," he said. "And very intelligent, too. They're known for seeking out company from our kind, but only on their own terms."

"You might say that," I said. "The day I arrived in Fairy Falls, he ambushed me and followed me home. Wouldn't take no for an answer."

"Sounds like a fairy cat," he said. "I'm glad you found yourself welcome here, Blair. It did cross my mind that staying in a community with no other fairies present would be lonely for you. I knew you'd be welcome among the witches, but still, I wondered how you were getting along."

Tears pricked my eyes. I'd imagined speaking to him for so long, the reality overwhelmed me. Even though we hadn't met face to face until this moment, we'd had a long journey together since he'd first contacted me when he'd heard about my presence in Fairy Falls after a deranged wizard had tried to kill me. We'd exchanged notes via pixie for months, enough for him to get a feel for my personality. And my penchant for attracting trouble, too. Maybe he *did* know me, better than I knew him, but there'd be time for me to get to know him.

My dad drew in a breath. "Blair, I wanted to tell you about your mother—"

"I know." My chest ached. "I wish I'd realised the Inquisitor was a fairy sooner, and that was why you couldn't tell me anything in your letters."

"I wish we'd been able to meet on the solstice, too," he said. "But I suspected it wouldn't be as easy as all that. There were too many complications."

"There were," I said. "Especially with the hunters. But we still managed to beat them."

"We did," he said. "I wish Tanith had been able to join us, too."

"I saw her ghost," I added. "Tanith, I mean. At the cottage. I spoke to her."

His expression softened. "You did?"

"On Samhain," I said. "When the veil was thin. My friend Rebecca was chosen as Head Witch... long story. Anyway, she was able to use the sceptre to help me speak to her."

"I'm glad you had that chance," he said. "It's one of my biggest regrets, that you had no time with your mother."

"Yeah." I blinked hard. "I always wondered... I mean, I heard she wasn't buried here in Fairy Falls. Another ghost told me. But she didn't say where."

"It was one thing I was able to arrange before my arrest," he said. "Come with me."

Confusion rose within me, but I walked with him along the path and into the forest. "We can see the falls later, if you like. Since that's where we were supposed to meet on the solstice."

"I'd like that," he said. "I imagine the town has changed a fair bit since I was last here."

"I bet," I said. "I hope the other fairies will feel safe coming back here now."

"What about the family you grew up with?" he asked. "Were they kind?"

"Yeah." I drew in a breath. "Mr and Mrs Wilkes are great. They don't know about the paranormal world, but you can meet them if you use your human glamour. I'd love for you to get to know one another. I think you'd like them."

I'd tell him about the goblin fruit debacle later. I had months of tales to tell, but for now, I was content to walk with him through the forest until the trees thinned a little and the sunlight broke through until I recognised my surroundings.

"We're going to Conor Underwood's house?" I asked.

"You met him?" he said. "Right, he gave you the Seeing Stone."

"Yeah," I said. "We didn't trust one another at first, but he eventually gave me the Seeing Stone, and now he's going to help us welcome the other fairies back to town."

We walked for several more minutes before we came to Conor's overgrown garden. He must have already heard us coming, because he stood outside the cottage waiting for us.

"Braden." He bowed his head in my father's direction. "I'm sorry, Braden. I kept the Seeing Stone, as I promised you, but I nearly failed to give it to Blair when she needed it."

"You didn't fail, clearly," he said. "It sounds like you're working hard to make this place safer for our fellow fairies."

"Of course," he murmured. "Tell me what you need from me, and it would be my honour to provide it."

He spoke like he truly was addressing a Prince, and it disconcerted me.

When my dad spoke, though, all he said was, "I wanted to take Blair to visit her mother's grave."

"Of course," said Conor. "We'll talk later."

He bowed to my dad, which if anything, befuddled me even more. *Please tell me people won't start bowing to me now.* That was all I needed.

"Grave?" I said. "Where?"

"This way." My dad led the way around the cottage and into Conor's back garden, which ended in a thicket of brambles. As we approached, an opening appeared in the tangle of branches, expanding into a doorway big enough for a person to step through, which lead into a field surrounded by hedges.

Inside the field stood a marble tomb, white and gleaming under the sun. My dad walked up to the tomb and halted in front of it. Silence surrounded us, cementing the impression of being cut off from the world at large.

"This is where your mother was buried," he said, his voice low. "Conor had her buried here at my request, where she would have wanted to be."

"It's lovely." I looked at the grave until it swam before my eyes, and Dad hugged me as I cried.

I wiped my eyes. "Next Samhain, maybe we can both see her together."

"I'd like that, Blair," he said.

We left the tomb behind and returned to the forest, heading back to the path into the town. I told him tales of my life in Fairy Falls as we walked. I had a lot to get through, almost a year of misadventures and discoveries, magic lessons and brushes with death.

As we reached the path by the lake again, I spotted a familiar group of individuals at the foot of the hill. *Nathan.*

Not just Nathan, but Mr Harker, too... and his children. Erin gave me a wave, Buck standing at her side. I waved back awkwardly, and my dad gave me a questioning look.

"Do you know those people?" he asked.

"Yeah." I picked up the pace, meeting them halfway up the hill. "Dad, this is my boyfriend, Nathan. And... and his family."

His brows rose as he took in Nathan and the others. "I'm Braden Eventide, but I expect you know that, given that I recognise at least one of you from the day I was jailed."

Mr Harker stepped in first. "I wanted to formally apologise to you for your incarceration at the hands of the Inquisitor and the hunters."

My mouth fell open, and I hastened to close it. The two of them looked at one another for a moment as though sizing each other up.

"I accept your apology," my dad replied, and a knot loosened in my chest. "Rowe Clearwater has held the hunters in his grip for too long. I'm glad he is no longer in charge."

"Have you heard from him?" I asked Nathan and the others. "The Inquisitor?"

"No," said Nathan. "None of us has. We think he's left the country."

"Or gone back to the fairy realm," said Dad. "It's been a few years, but I wouldn't expect him to give up entirely, even in defeat."

"Don't get arrested again," I said firmly. "It took me long enough to get you out last time."

Mr Harker cleared his throat. "The Inquisitor no longer leads the hunters, and so we no longer support him. We would also like to offer you our Pixie-Glass, if you like, since it rightfully belongs to the fairies."

"Seriously?" I looked at my dad. "That's up to you. I'd like to think we won't be forced to communicate from behind bars again anytime soon."

"Not if we have anything to do with it," said Erin. "Nice to meet you, Blair's dad. And you met the cat, too? Cute, isn't he?"

"Miaow," said Sky, glaring at Nathan's dad. I guessed he hadn't quite forgotten how Nathan's family had treated the pair of us when we'd first met. In fairness, neither had I. It'd be a long time before I'd be able to look at Mr Harker without remembering everything he'd done to me and my family, and we'd probably never be friendly with one another. Yet now we had a chance to mend things between us, I wouldn't pass it up. Not when my dad seemed genuinely open to forgiving them. If it helped him accept Nathan as my boyfriend, so much the better.

"Anyway, we'll leave you to it," said Nathan. "It's great to meet you, Mr Eventide."

As the two of us walked out of earshot, Dad turned to me. "That young man… you're dating one of the hunters?"

"He left them years ago," I said. "But yeah… Nathan used to be a hunter, a while ago. Is that okay?"

"You're old enough to make your own decisions," he said. "If anything, it's a good sign for our future. For both the fairies and the hunters."

"I didn't know he was a hunter at first," I added. "I didn't know I was a fairy, either. I still don't really get on with his dad or brothers, but his dad did help me against the Inquisitor in the end. I understand if you don't forgive them for that."

"Why wouldn't I?" he said. "The man calling himself Inquisitor Hare wove his spell over the hunters for years, and I'd gladly accept the apologies of anyone who has willingly turned their backs on him."

"I guess the hunters will have to change without him there." Hopefully for the better.

"Things have a habit of working themselves out," he said. "With a little encouragement."

"You know what?" I said. "They do."

We had years to catch up on, countless conversations to have, and it wouldn't always be easy. But we'd face everything that came our way together—as a family.

ABOUT THE AUTHOR

Elle Adams lives in the middle of England, where she spends most of her time reading an ever-growing mountain of books, planning her next adventure, or writing. Elle's books are humorous mysteries with a paranormal twist, packed with magical mayhem.

She also writes urban and contemporary fantasy novels as Emma L. Adams.

Find out more about Elle's books at: https://www. elleadamsauthor.com/

Find Elle on Facebook at https://www.facebook. com/pg/ElleAdamsAuthor/

www.ingramcontent.com/pod-product-compliance
Lightning Source LLC
Chambersburg PA
CBHW020811190726
48285CB00006B/2241